W9-DDR-314

DreamWorks

HOW TO TRAIN YOUR

DRAGON

The Serpent's Heir

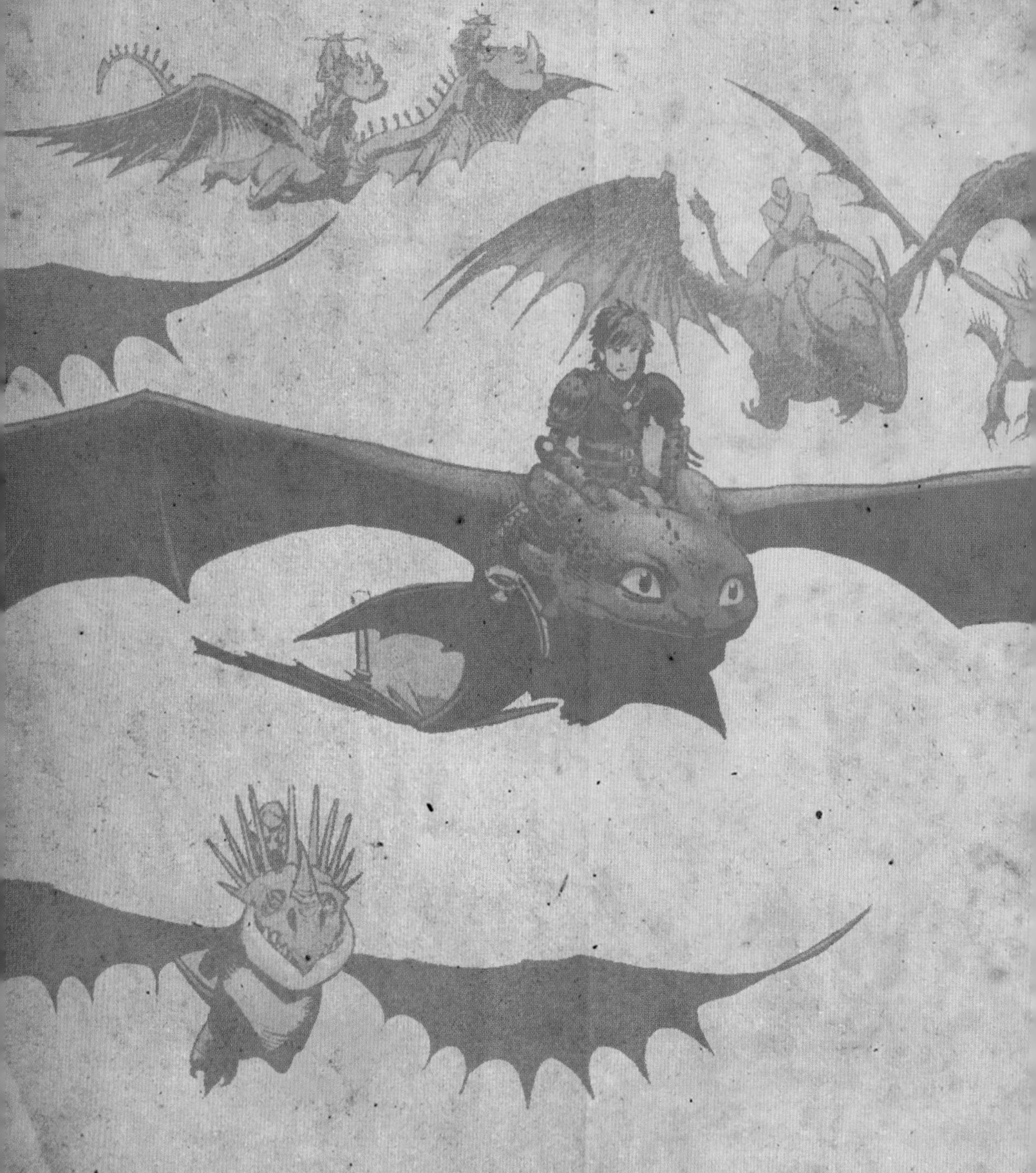

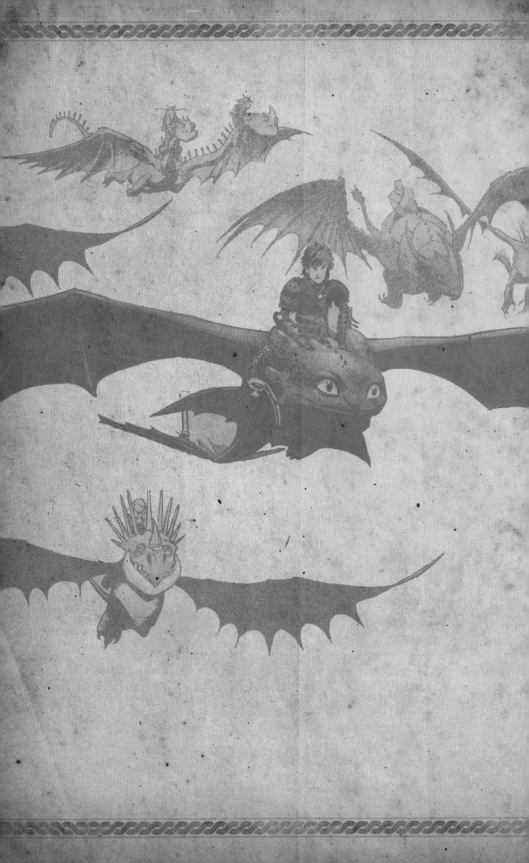

DreamWorks

HOW TO TRAIN YOUR
DRAGON

The Serpent's Heir

Script by
**Dean DeBlois &
Richard Hamilton**

Art by
Doug Wheatley

Coloring by
Wes Dzioba

Lettering by
Michael Heisler

Cover Art by
Pierre-Olivier Vincent (POV)

DARK HORSE BOOKS

PRESIDENT AND PUBLISHER
Mike Richardson

EDITOR
Randy Stradley

ASSISTANT EDITORS
Kevin Burkhalter
AND **Freddye Miller**

COLLECTION DESIGNER
David Nestelle

DIGITAL ART TECHNICIAN
Christina McKenzie

Special thanks to Bonnie Arnold, Elizabeth C. Camp, Corinne Combs, Lawrence "Shifty" Hamashima, Kate Spencer Lachance, Barbara Layman, Megan Startz, Mike Sund, John Tanzer, Joe Vance, and Pierre-Olivier Vincent (POV) at DreamWorks Animation.

How To Train Your Dragon: The Serpent's Heir

How To Train Your Dragon © 2017 DreamWorks Animation LLC.
All Rights Reserved. Dark Horse Books® and the Dark Horse logo are registered trademarks of Dark Horse Comics, Inc. All rights reserved. No portion of this publication may be reproduced or transmitted, in any form or by any means, without the express written permission of Dark Horse Comics, Inc. Names, characters, places, and incidents featured in this publication either are the product of the author's imagination or are used fictitiously. Any resemblance to actual persons (living or dead), events, institutions, or locales, without satiric intent, is coincidental.

Published by Dark Horse Books
A division of Dark Horse Comics, Inc.
10956 SE Main Street
Milwaukie, OR 97222

DarkHorse.com

International Licensing: 503-905-2377
To find a comics shop in your area, call the
Comic Shop Locator Service toll-free at 1-888-266-4226.

First edition: February 2017
ISBN 978-1-61655-931-1

1 3 5 7 9 10 8 6 4 2
Printed in China

THIS STORY TAKES PLACE
SHORTLY AFTER THE EVENTS IN THE FILM
How To Train Your Dragon 2

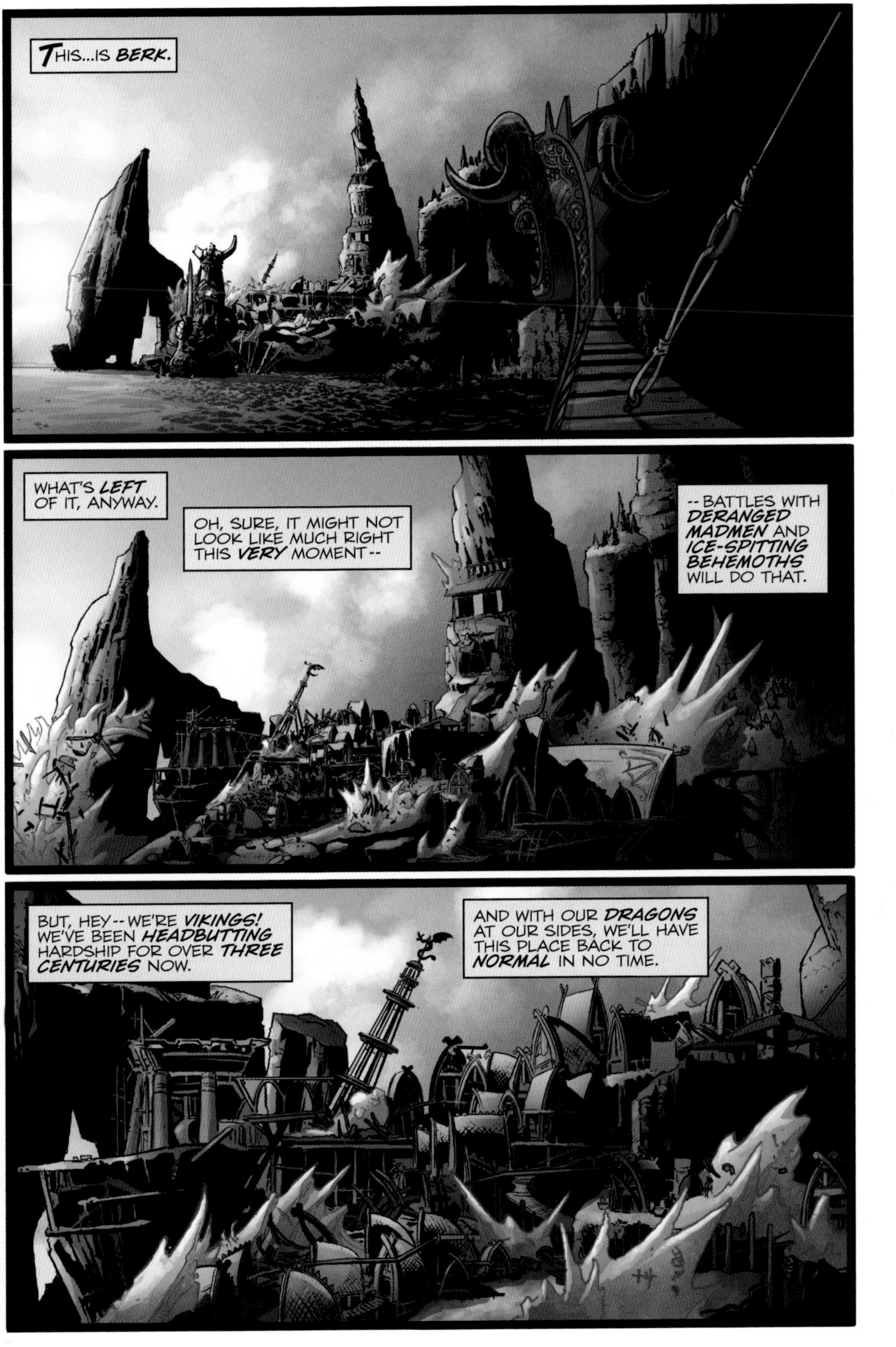
THIS...IS BERK.
WHAT'S LEFT OF IT, ANYWAY.
OH, SURE, IT MIGHT NOT LOOK LIKE MUCH RIGHT THIS VERY MOMENT--
--BATTLES WITH DERANGED MADMEN AND ICE-SPITTING BEHEMOTHS WILL DO THAT.
BUT, HEY--WE'RE VIKINGS! WE'VE BEEN HEADBUTTING HARDSHIP FOR OVER THREE CENTURIES NOW.
AND WITH OUR DRAGONS AT OUR SIDES, WE'LL HAVE THIS PLACE BACK TO NORMAL IN NO TIME.

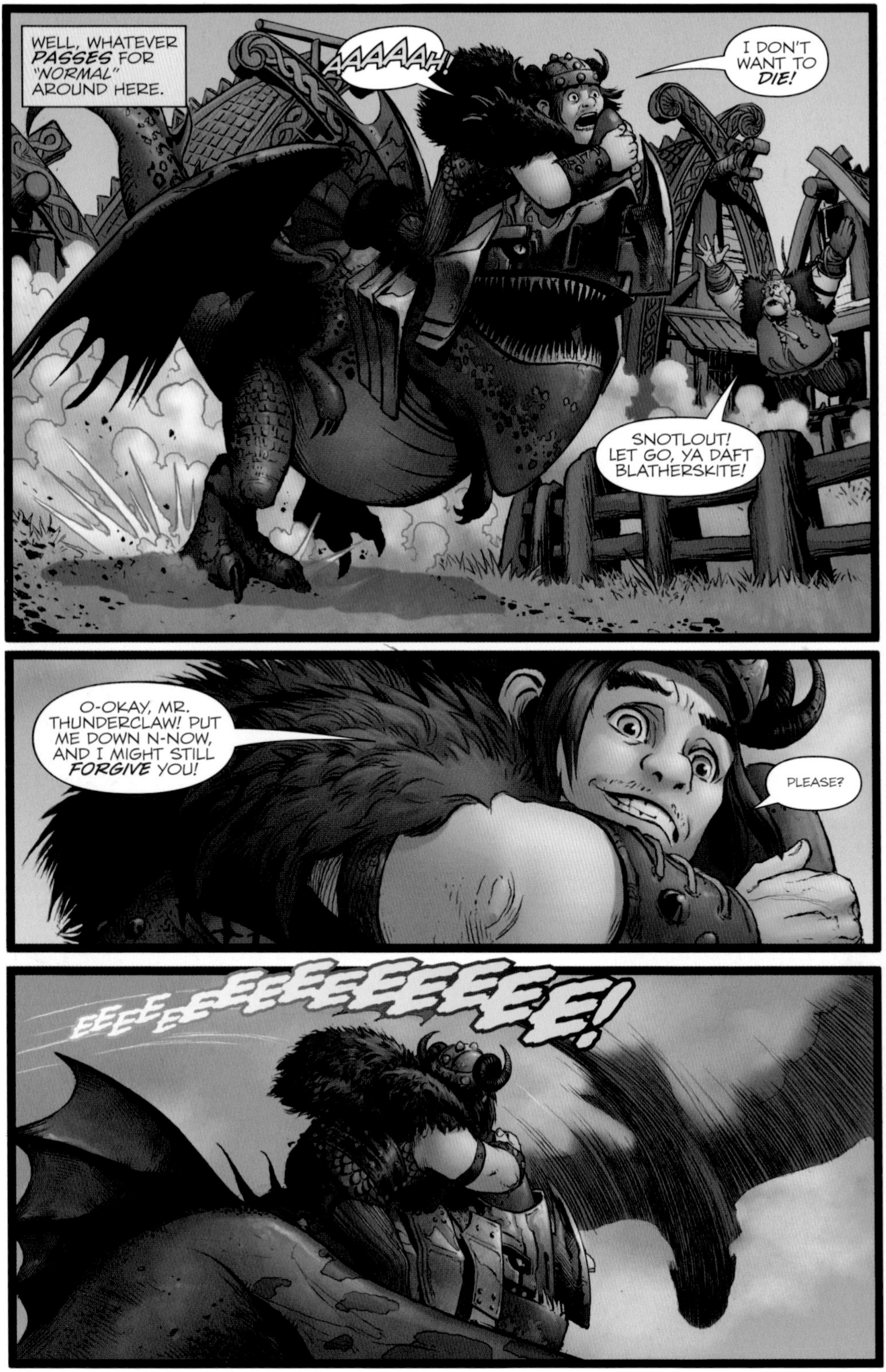
WELL, WHATEVER PASSES FOR "NORMAL" AROUND HERE.
AAAAAH!
I DON'T WANT TO DIE!
SNOTLOUT! LET GO, YA DAFT BLATHERSKITE!
O-OKAY, MR. THUNDERCLAW! PUT ME DOWN N-NOW, AND I MIGHT STILL FORGIVE YOU!
PLEASE?
EEEEEEEEEEEEEEEEEE!

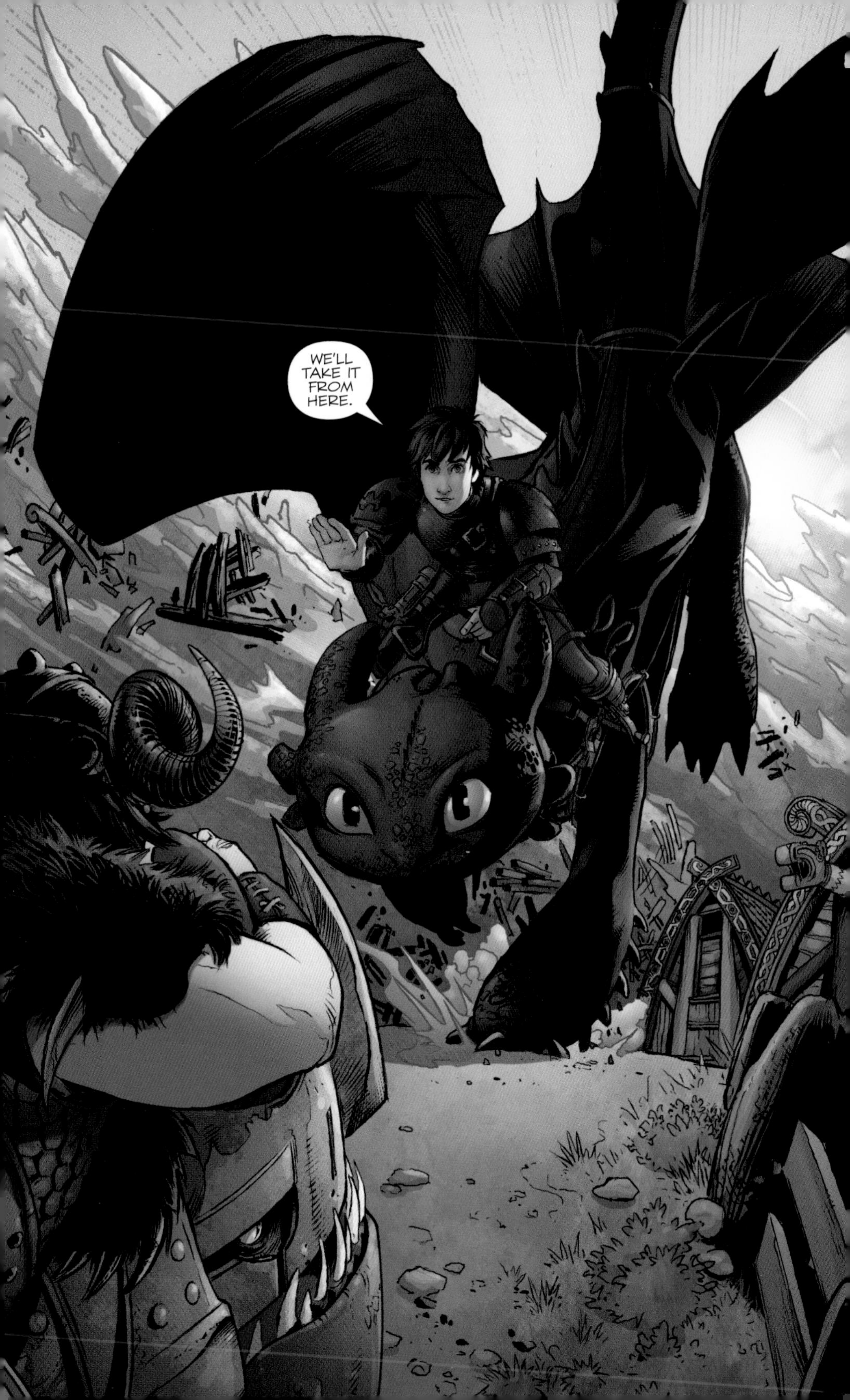
WE'LL TAKE IT FROM HERE.

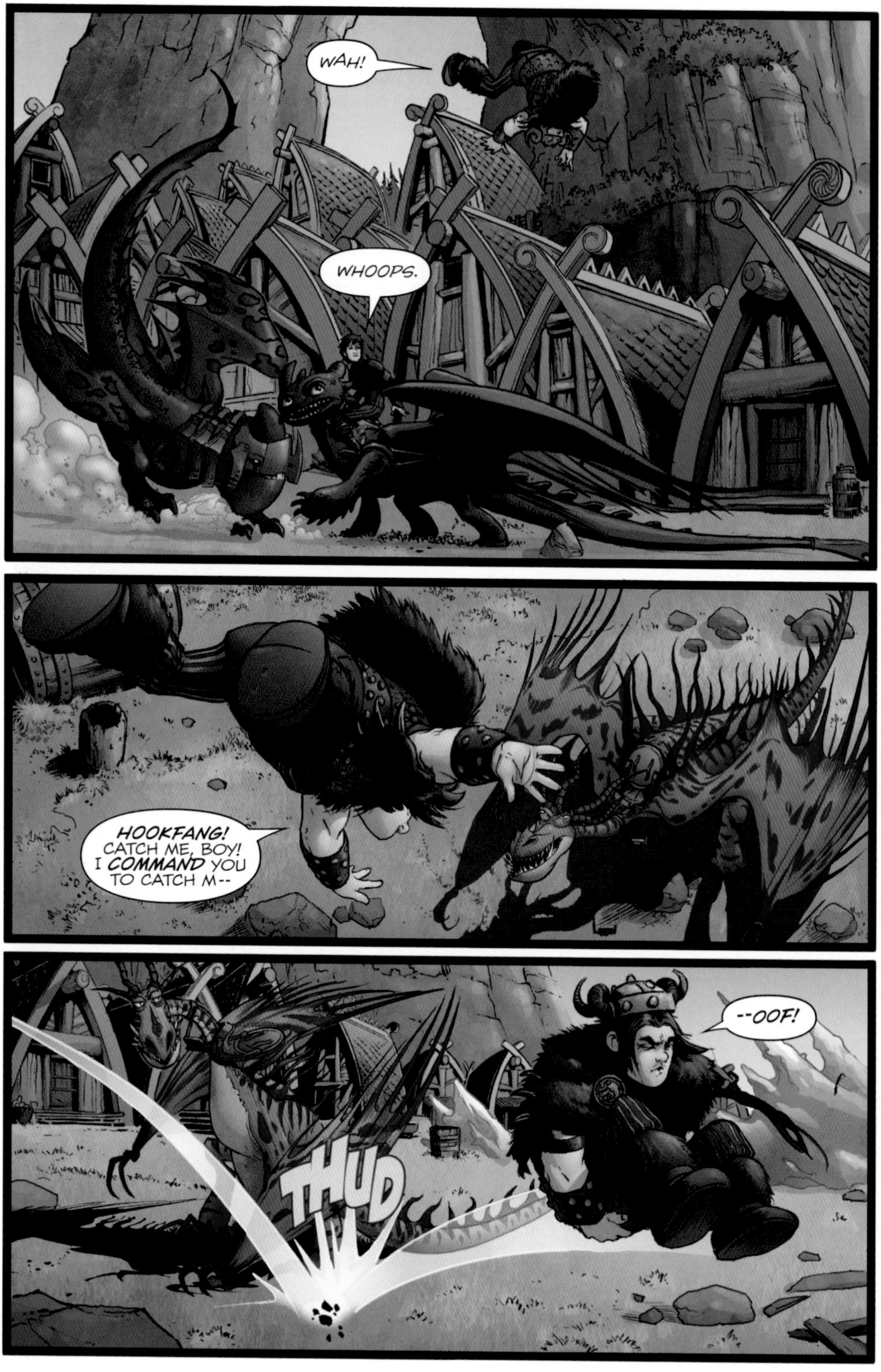
WAH!
WHOOPS.
HOOKFANG! CATCH ME, BOY! I COMMAND YOU TO CATCH M--
THUD
--OOF!

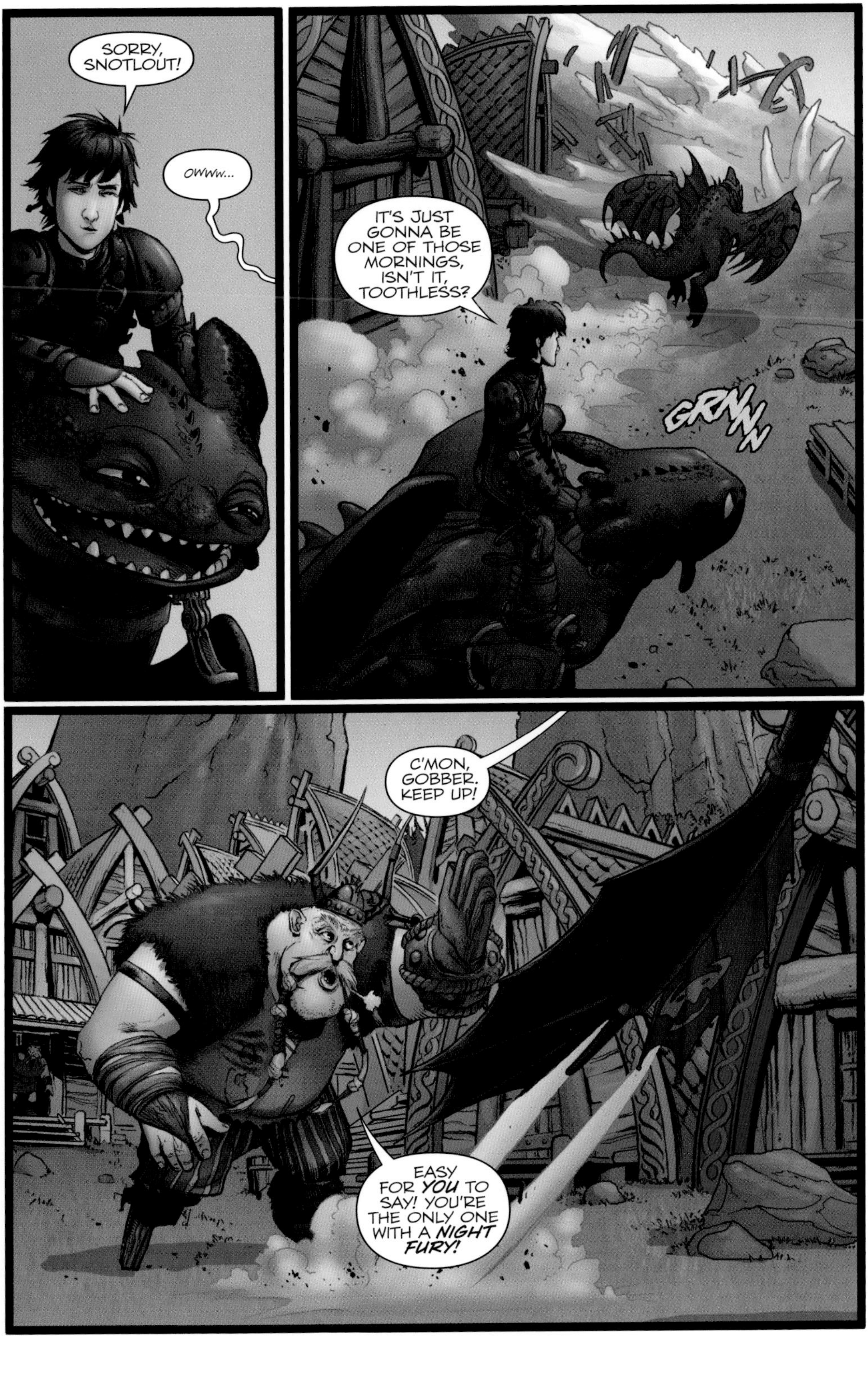
SORRY, SNOTLOUT!
OWWW...
IT'S JUST GONNA BE ONE OF THOSE MORNINGS, ISN'T IT, TOOTHLESS?
GRNNN
C'MON, GOBBER. KEEP UP!
EASY FOR ***YOU*** TO SAY! YOU'RE THE ONLY ONE WITH A ***NIGHT FURY!***

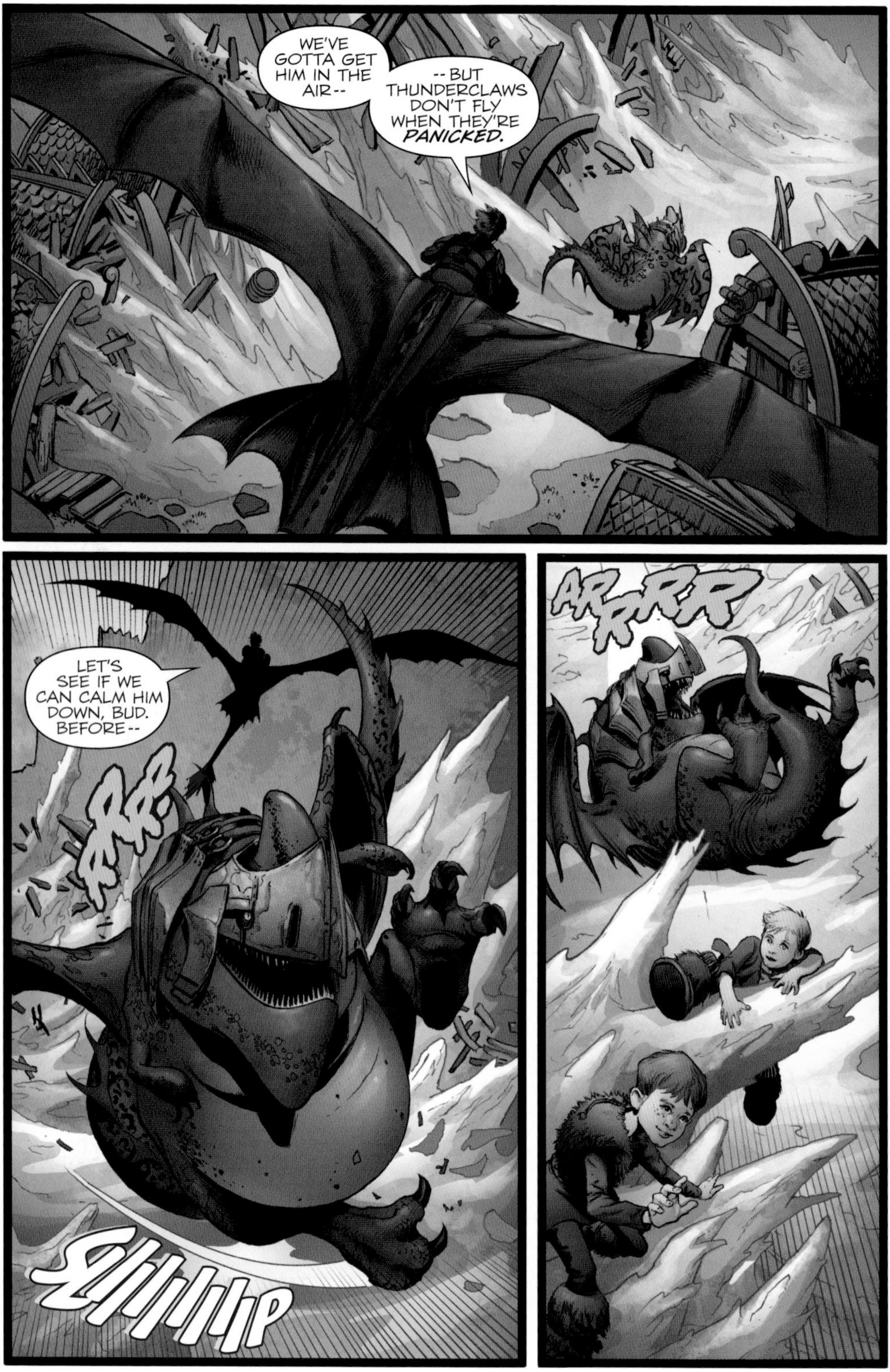
WE'VE GOTTA GET HIM IN THE AIR--
--BUT THUNDERCLAWS DON'T FLY WHEN THEY'RE *PANICKED.*
LET'S SEE IF WE CAN CALM HIM DOWN, BUD. BEFORE--

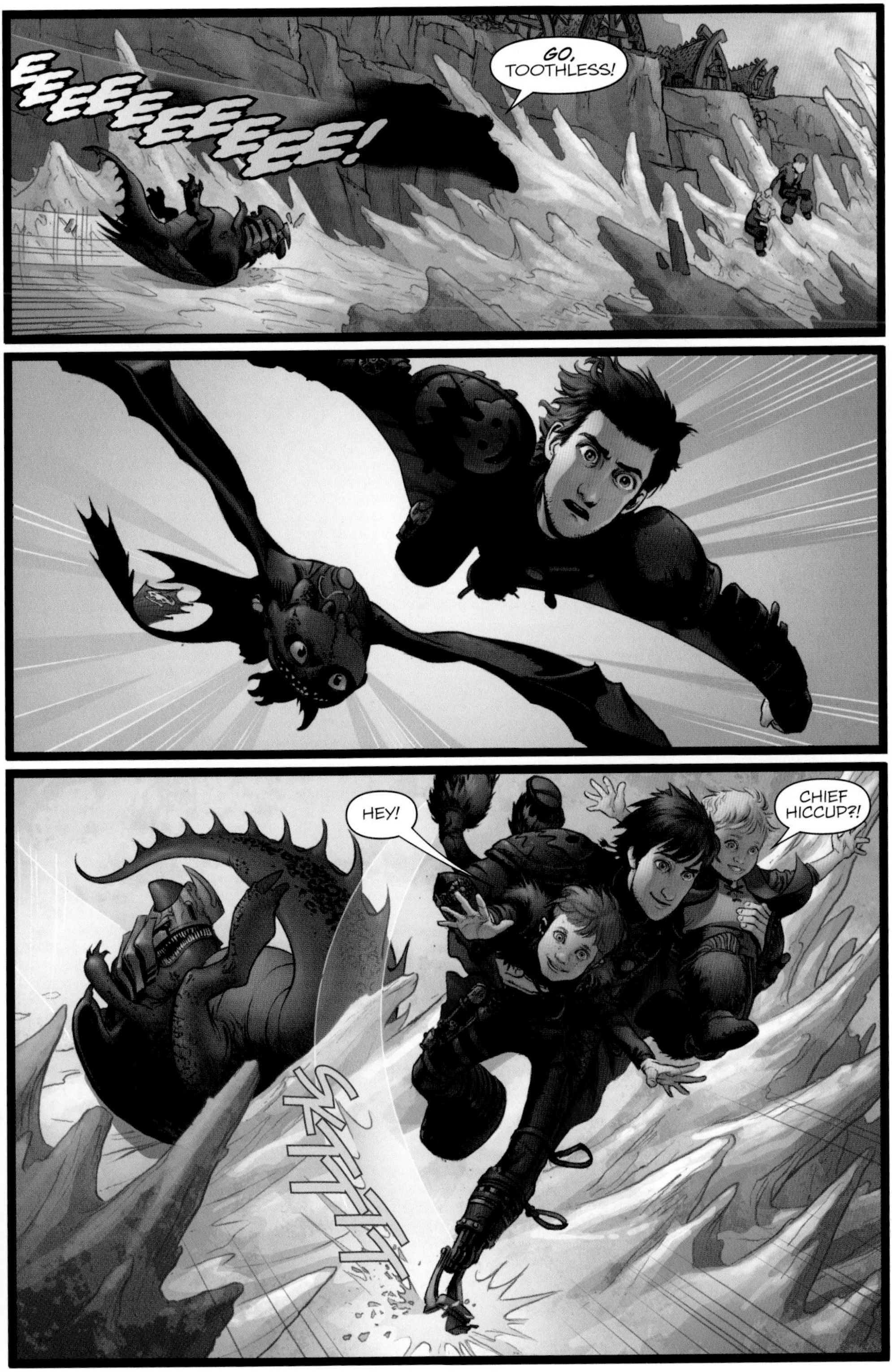
EEEEEEEEEEE!
GO, TOOTHLESS!
HEY!
CHIEF HICCUP?!
SKTTTT

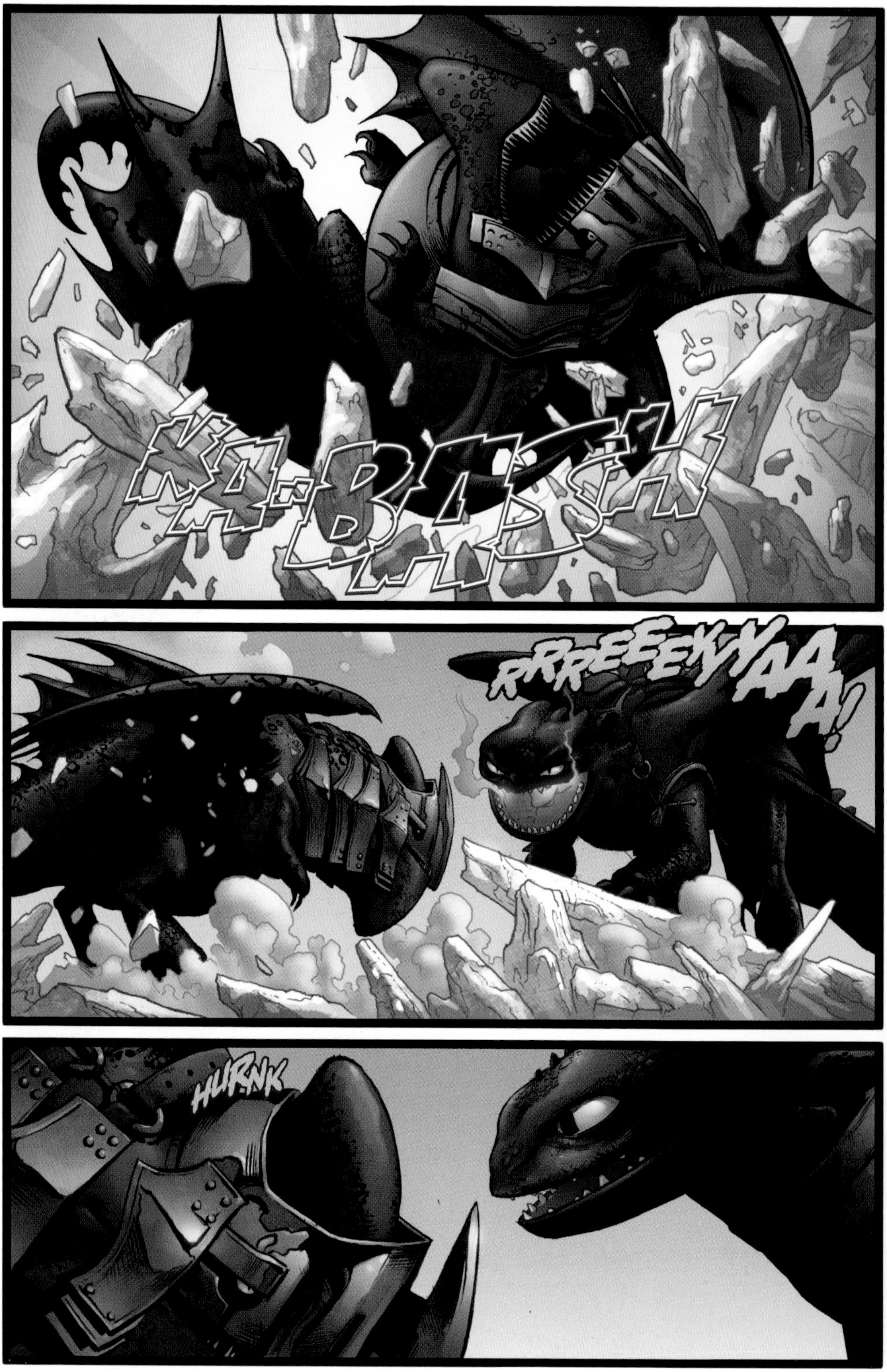
KA-BLASH
RRREEEKYAAA!
HURNK

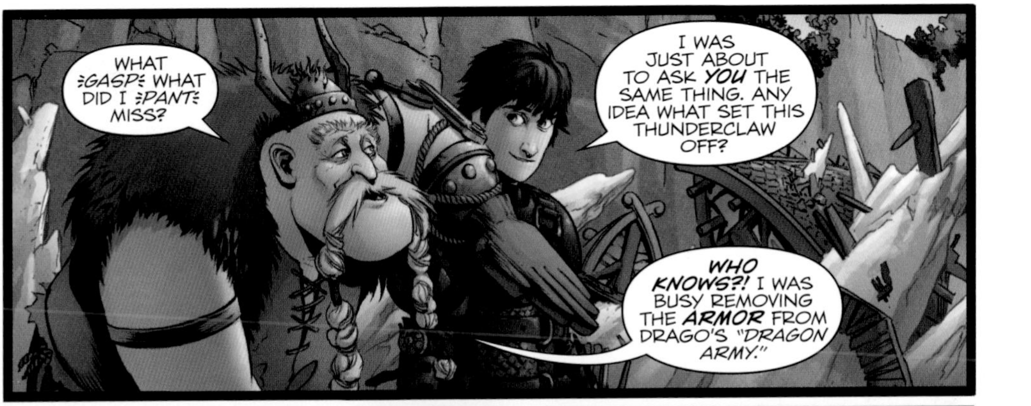
WHAT ⁝GASP⁝ WHAT DID I ⁝PANT⁝ MISS?
I WAS JUST ABOUT TO ASK YOU THE SAME THING. ANY IDEA WHAT SET THIS THUNDERCLAW OFF?
WHO KNOWS?! I WAS BUSY REMOVING THE ARMOR FROM DRAGO'S "DRAGON ARMY."

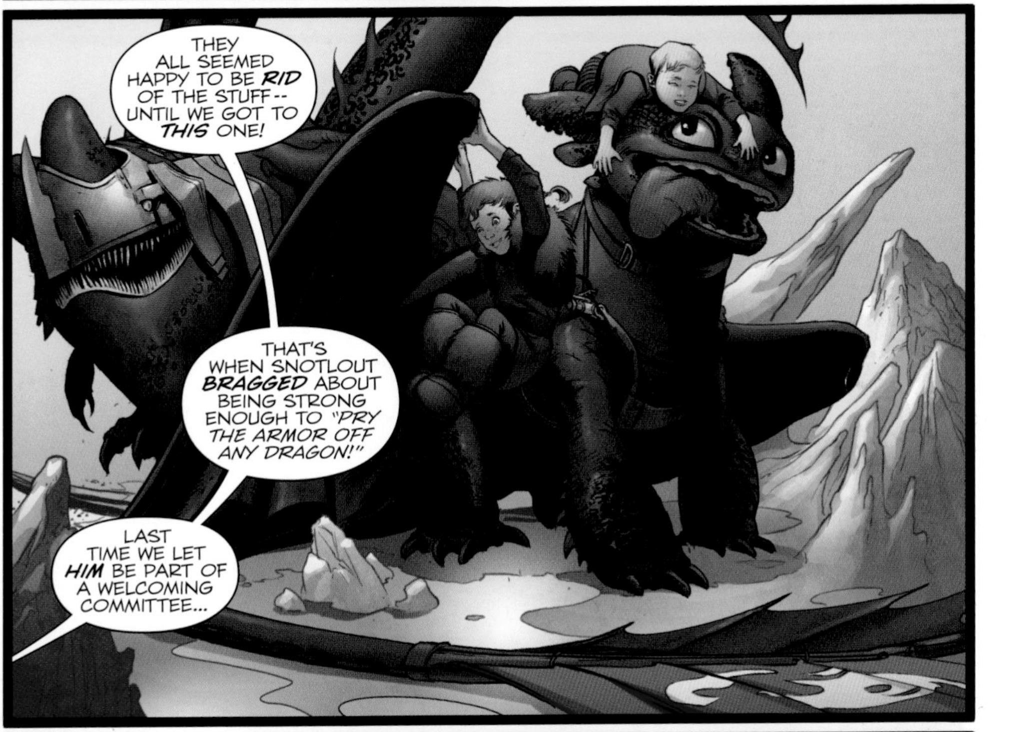
THEY ALL SEEMED HAPPY TO BE RID OF THE STUFF-- UNTIL WE GOT TO THIS ONE!
THAT'S WHEN SNOTLOUT BRAGGED ABOUT BEING STRONG ENOUGH TO "PRY THE ARMOR OFF ANY DRAGON!"
LAST TIME WE LET HIM BE PART OF A WELCOMING COMMITTEE...

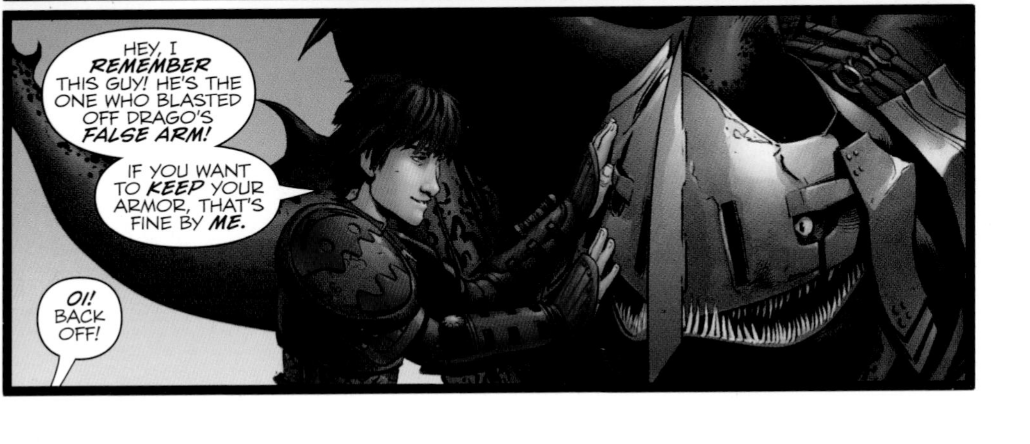
HEY, I REMEMBER THIS GUY! HE'S THE ONE WHO BLASTED OFF DRAGO'S FALSE ARM!
IF YOU WANT TO KEEP YOUR ARMOR, THAT'S FINE BY ME.
OI! BACK OFF!

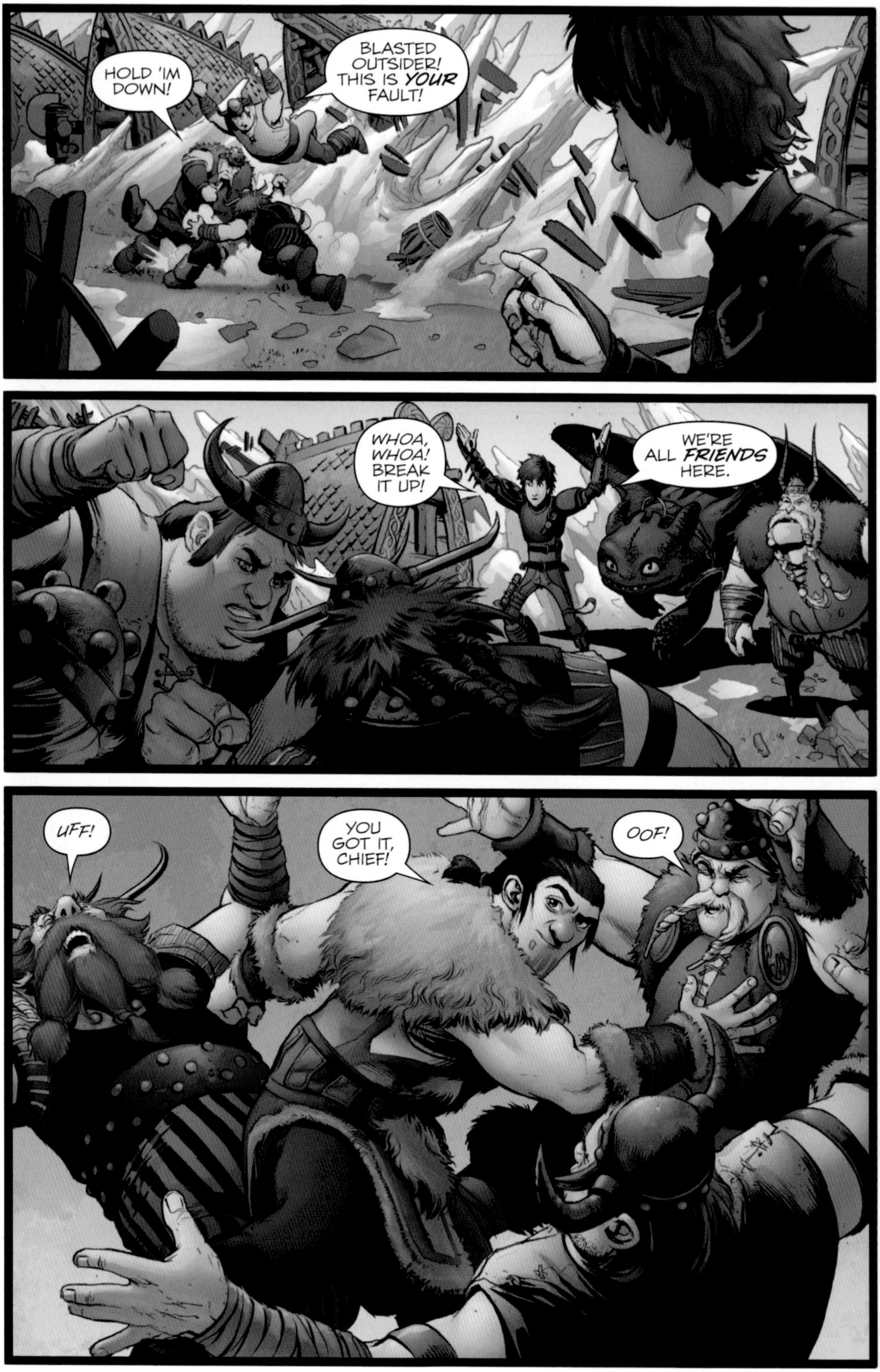
HOLD 'IM DOWN!
BLASTED OUTSIDER! THIS IS *YOUR* FAULT!
WHOA, WHOA! BREAK IT UP!
WE'RE ALL *FRIENDS* HERE.
UFF!
YOU GOT IT, CHIEF!
OOF!

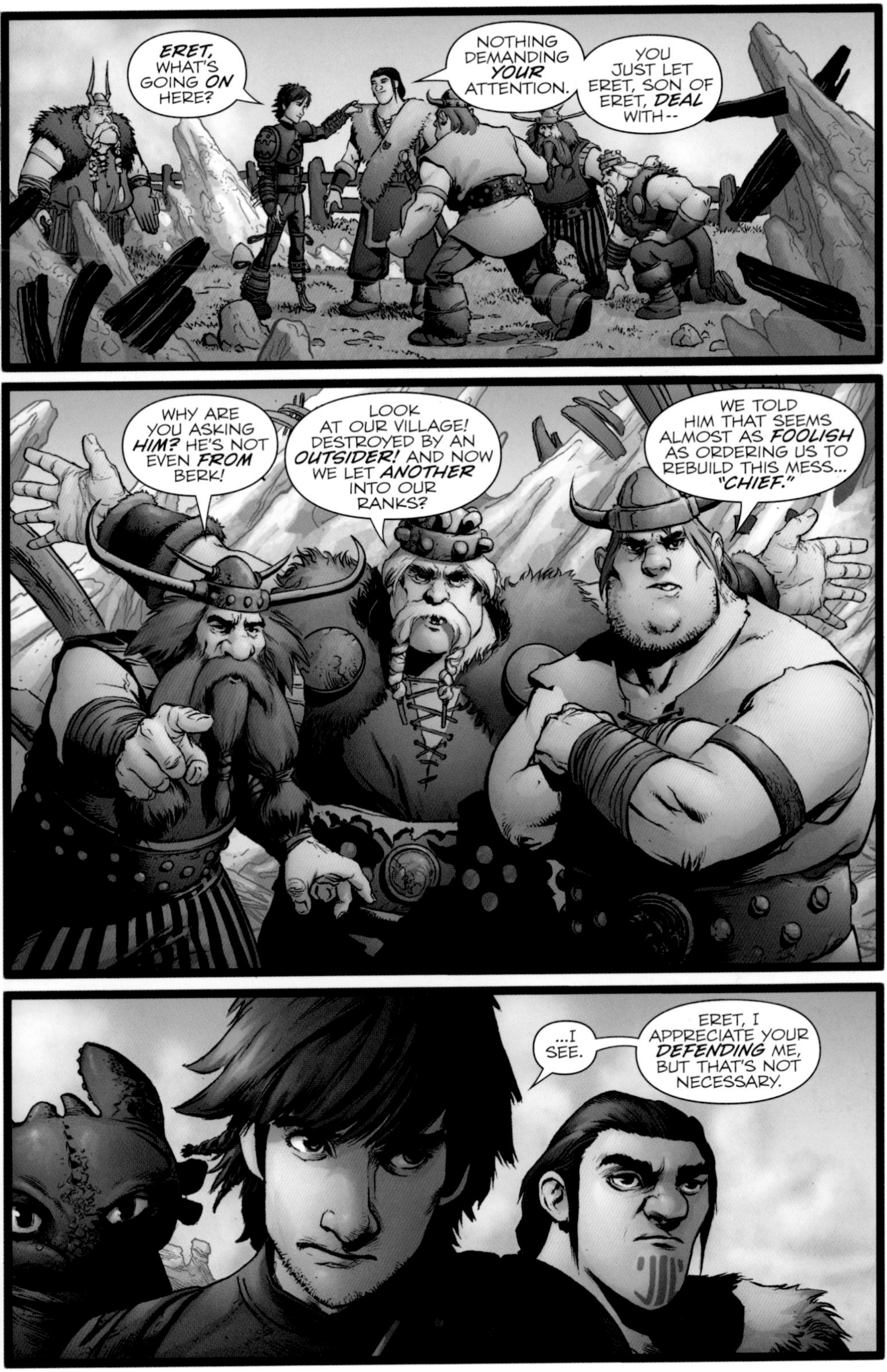
ERET, WHAT'S GOING ON HERE?
NOTHING DEMANDING YOUR ATTENTION.
YOU JUST LET ERET, SON OF ERET, DEAL WITH--
WHY ARE YOU ASKING HIM? HE'S NOT EVEN FROM BERK!
LOOK AT OUR VILLAGE! DESTROYED BY AN OUTSIDER! AND NOW WE LET ANOTHER INTO OUR RANKS?
WE TOLD HIM THAT SEEMS ALMOST AS FOOLISH AS ORDERING US TO REBUILD THIS MESS... "CHIEF."
...I SEE.
ERET, I APPRECIATE YOUR DEFENDING ME, BUT THAT'S NOT NECESSARY.

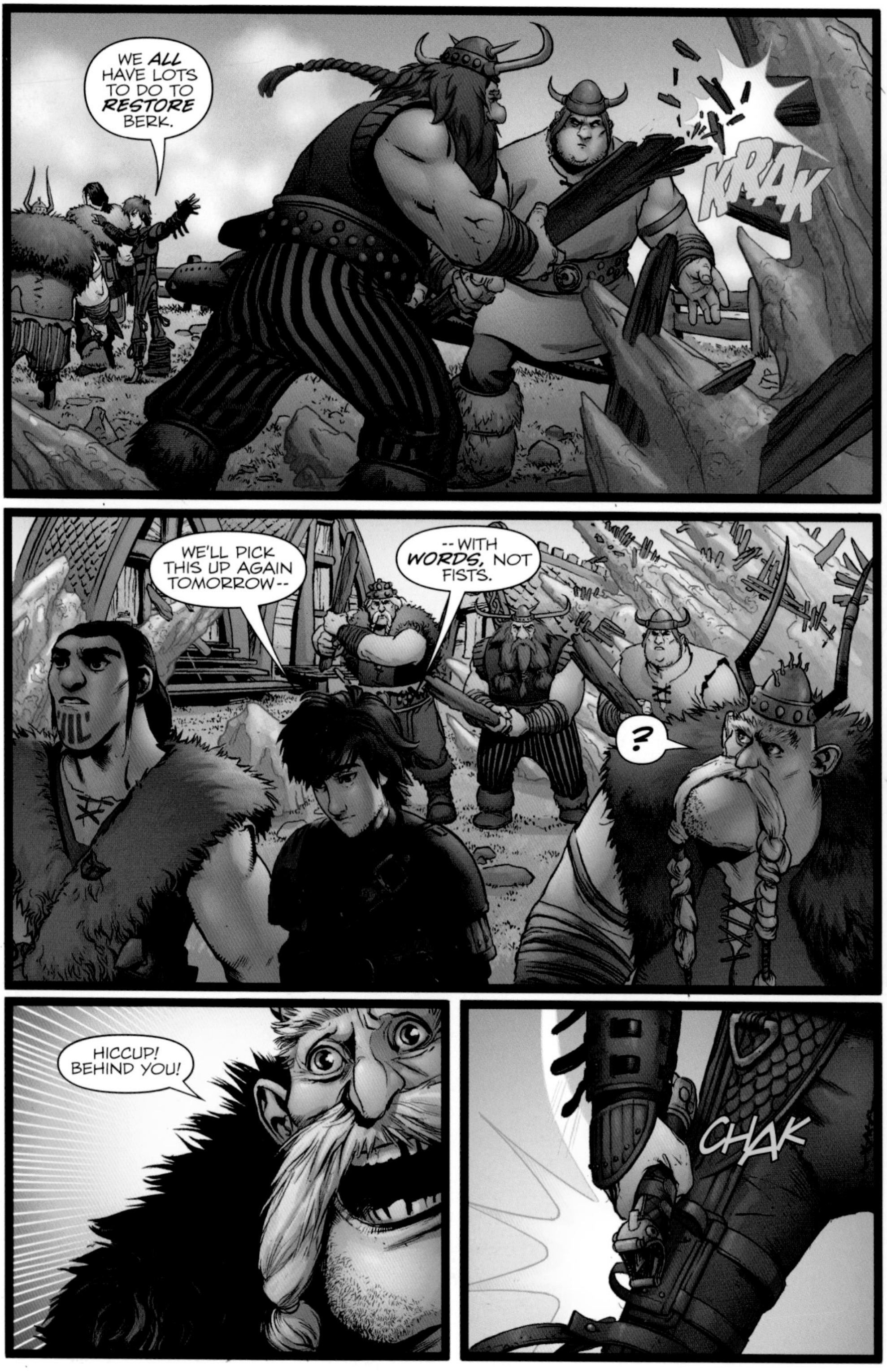
WE ALL HAVE LOTS TO DO TO RESTORE BERK.
KRAK
WE'LL PICK THIS UP AGAIN TOMORROW--
--WITH WORDS, NOT FISTS.
?
HICCUP! BEHIND YOU!
CHAK

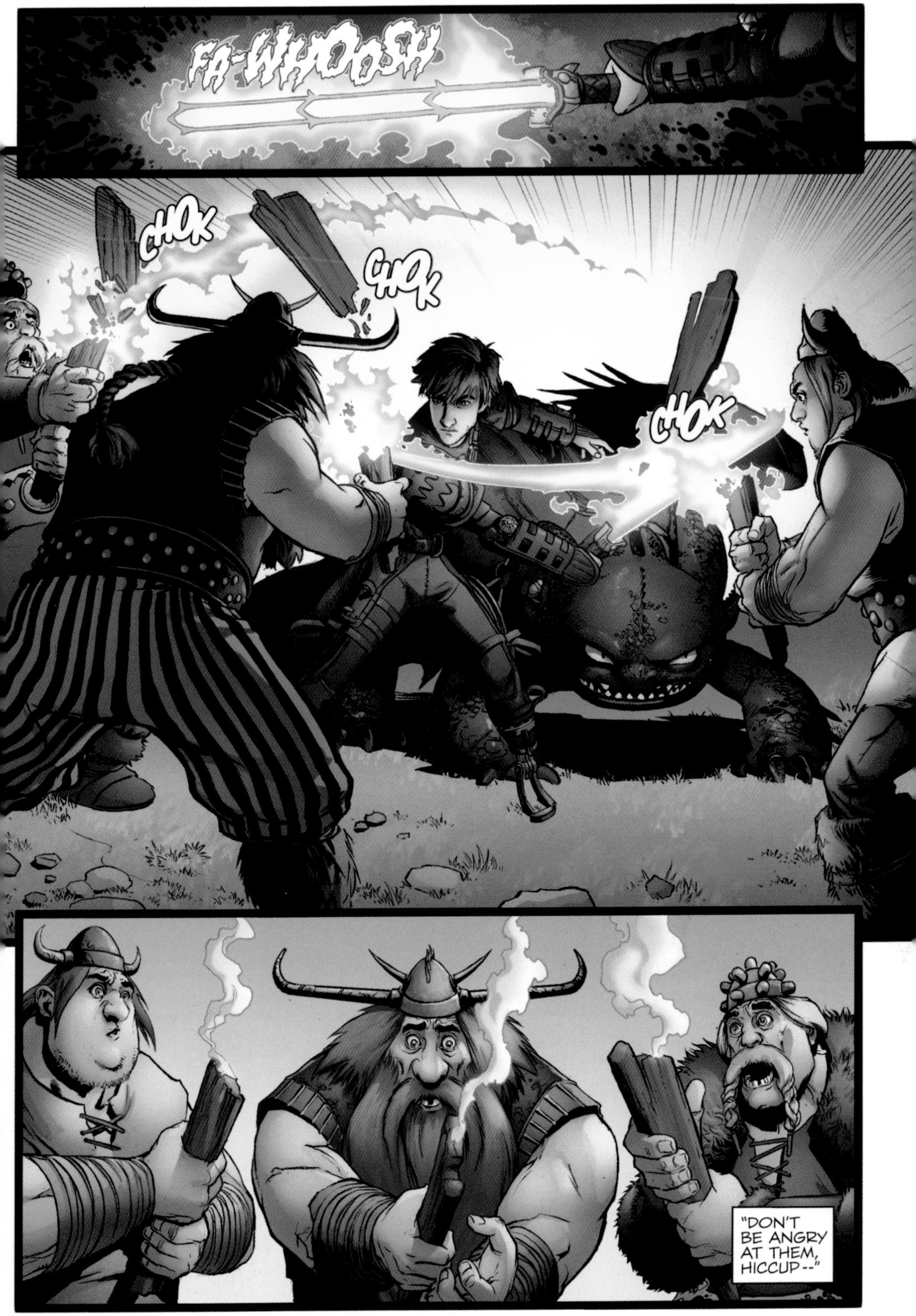
FA-WHOOSH
CHOK
CHOK
CHOK
"DON'T BE ANGRY AT THEM, HICCUP --"

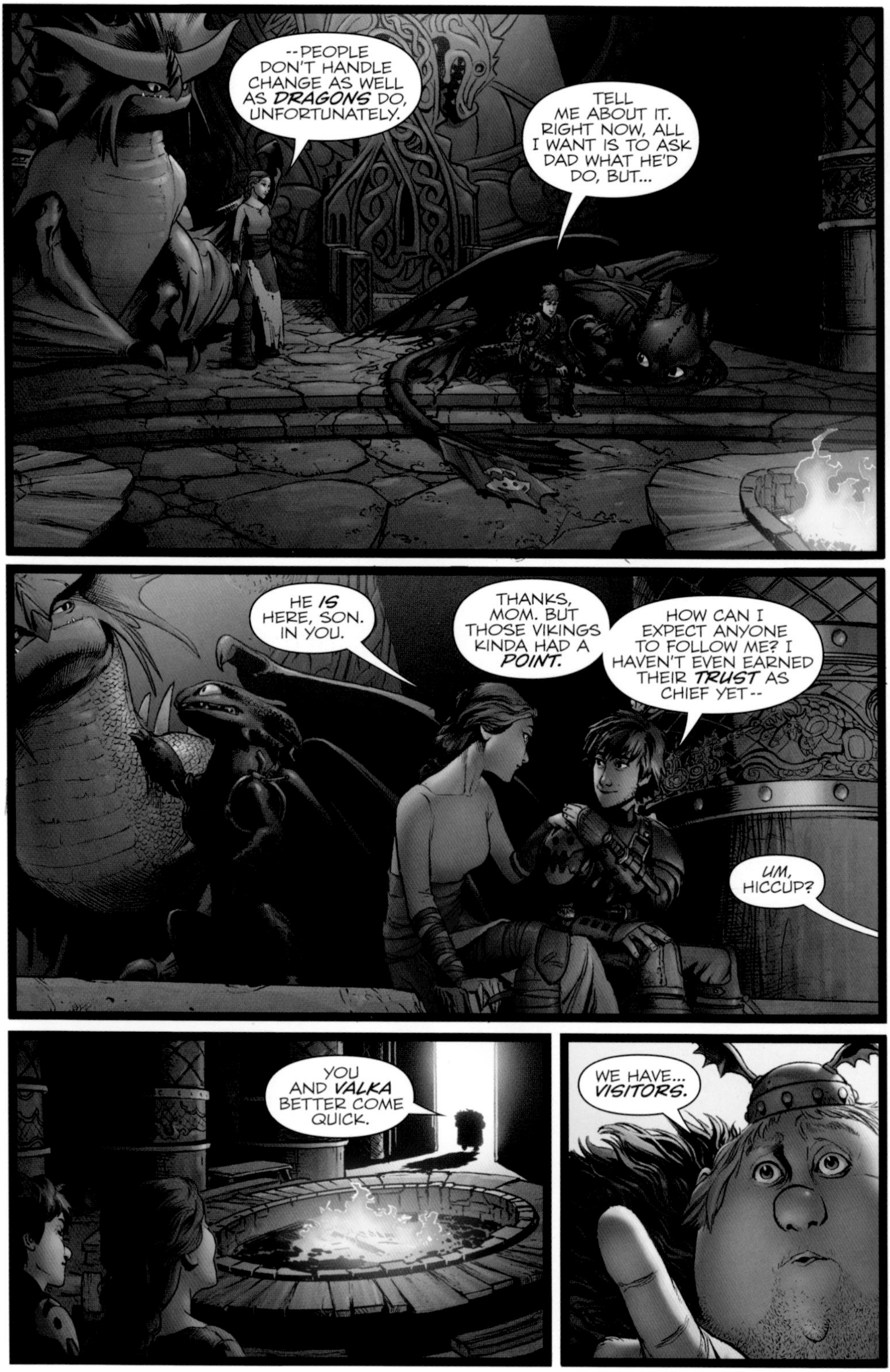
--PEOPLE DON'T HANDLE CHANGE AS WELL AS DRAGONS DO, UNFORTUNATELY.
TELL ME ABOUT IT. RIGHT NOW, ALL I WANT IS TO ASK DAD WHAT HE'D DO, BUT...
HE IS HERE, SON. IN YOU.
THANKS, MOM. BUT THOSE VIKINGS KINDA HAD A POINT.
HOW CAN I EXPECT ANYONE TO FOLLOW ME? I HAVEN'T EVEN EARNED THEIR TRUST AS CHIEF YET--
UM, HICCUP?
YOU AND VALKA BETTER COME QUICK.
WE HAVE... VISITORS.

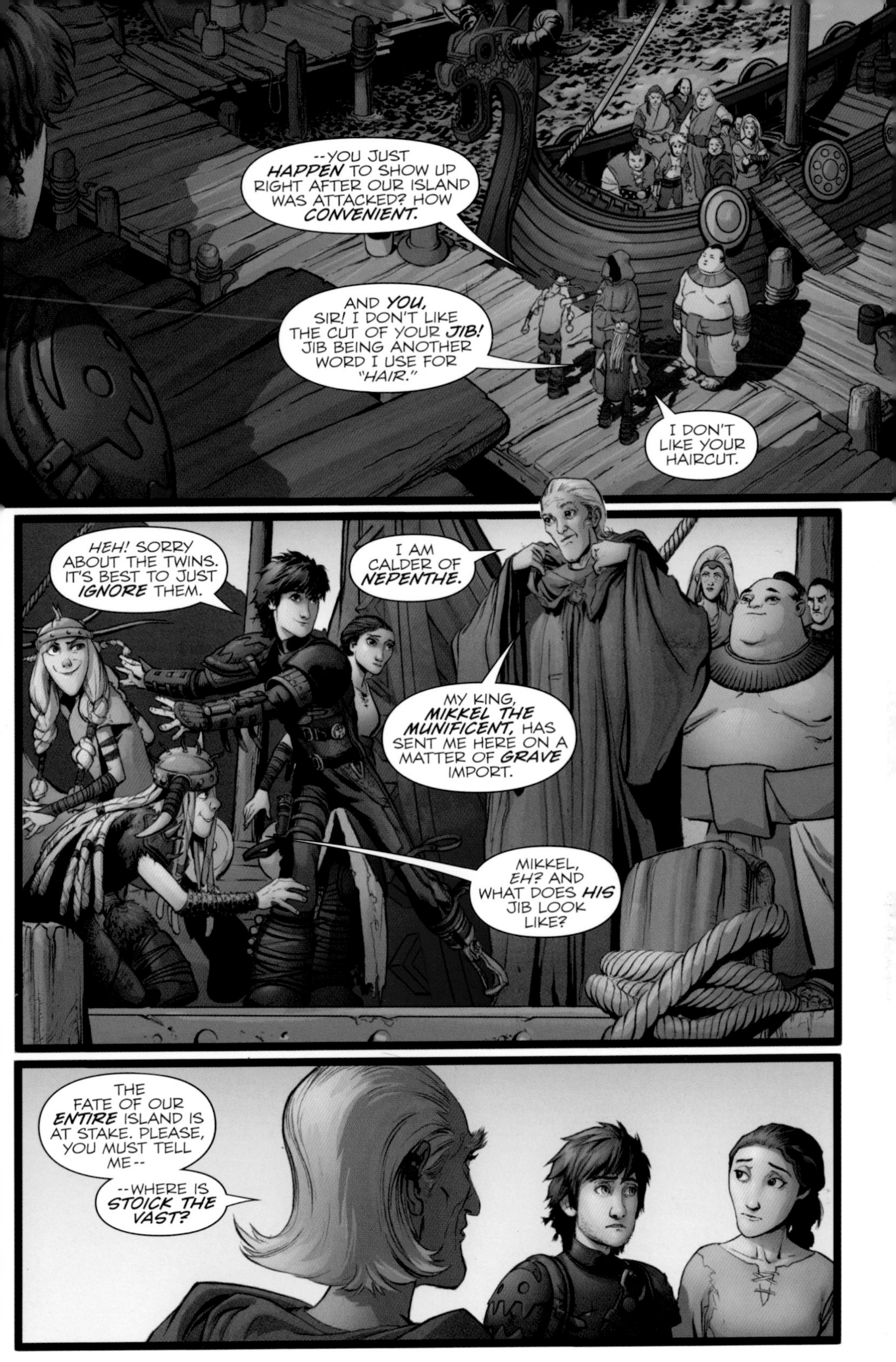
--YOU JUST HAPPEN TO SHOW UP RIGHT AFTER OUR ISLAND WAS ATTACKED? HOW CONVENIENT.
AND YOU, SIR! I DON'T LIKE THE CUT OF YOUR JIB! JIB BEING ANOTHER WORD I USE FOR "HAIR."
I DON'T LIKE YOUR HAIRCUT.
HEH! SORRY ABOUT THE TWINS. IT'S BEST TO JUST IGNORE THEM.
I AM CALDER OF NEPENTHE.
MY KING, MIKKEL THE MUNIFICENT, HAS SENT ME HERE ON A MATTER OF GRAVE IMPORT.
MIKKEL, EH? AND WHAT DOES HIS JIB LOOK LIKE?
THE FATE OF OUR ENTIRE ISLAND IS AT STAKE. PLEASE, YOU MUST TELL ME--
--WHERE IS STOICK THE VAST?

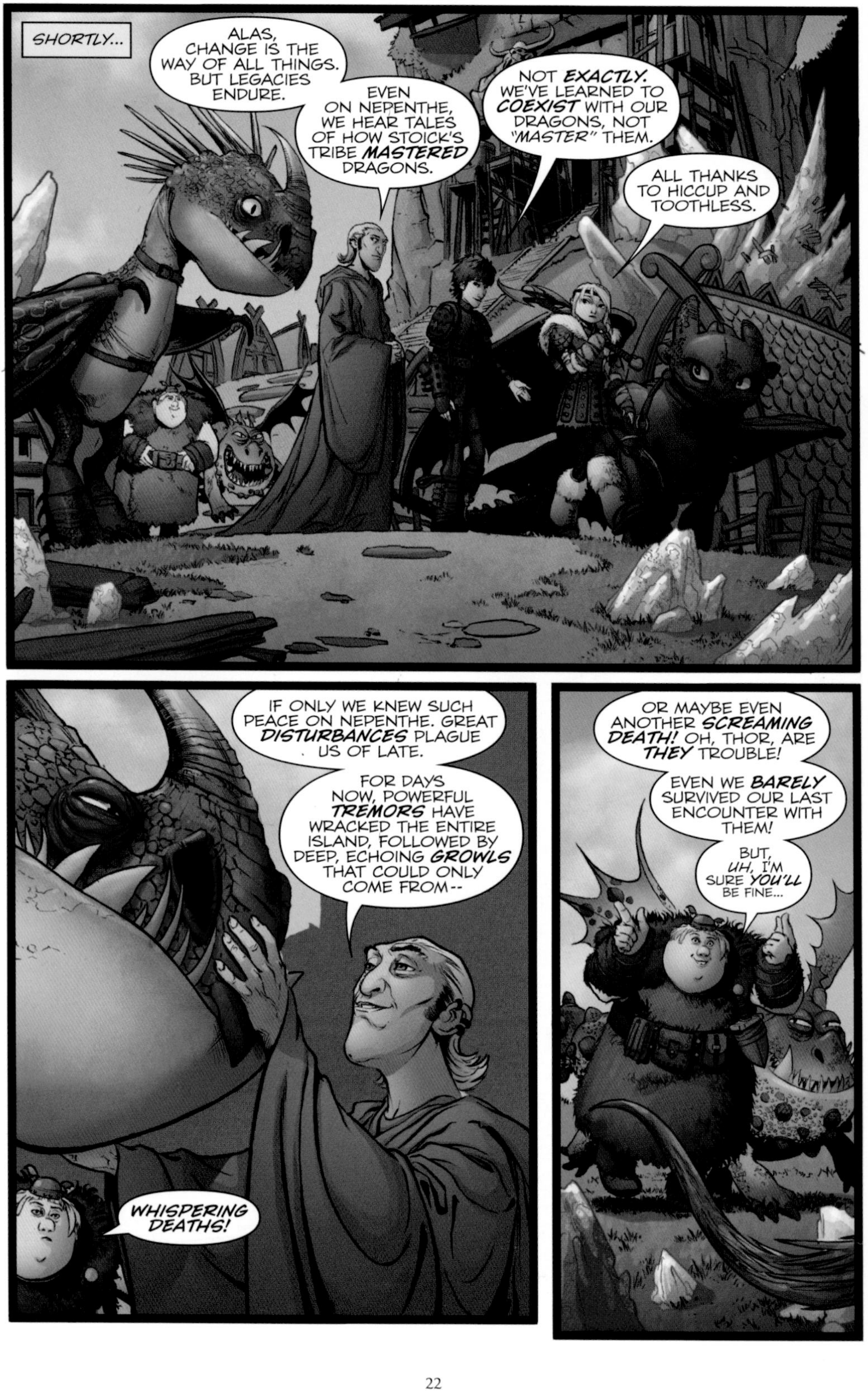
SHORTLY...
ALAS, CHANGE IS THE WAY OF ALL THINGS. BUT LEGACIES ENDURE.
EVEN ON NEPENTHE, WE HEAR TALES OF HOW STOICK'S TRIBE MASTERED DRAGONS.
NOT EXACTLY. WE'VE LEARNED TO COEXIST WITH OUR DRAGONS, NOT "MASTER" THEM.
ALL THANKS TO HICCUP AND TOOTHLESS.
IF ONLY WE KNEW SUCH PEACE ON NEPENTHE. GREAT DISTURBANCES PLAGUE US OF LATE.
FOR DAYS NOW, POWERFUL TREMORS HAVE WRACKED THE ENTIRE ISLAND, FOLLOWED BY DEEP, ECHOING GROWLS THAT COULD ONLY COME FROM--
WHISPERING DEATHS!
OR MAYBE EVEN ANOTHER SCREAMING DEATH! OH, THOR, ARE THEY TROUBLE!
EVEN WE BARELY SURVIVED OUR LAST ENCOUNTER WITH THEM!
BUT, UH, I'M SURE YOU'LL BE FINE...

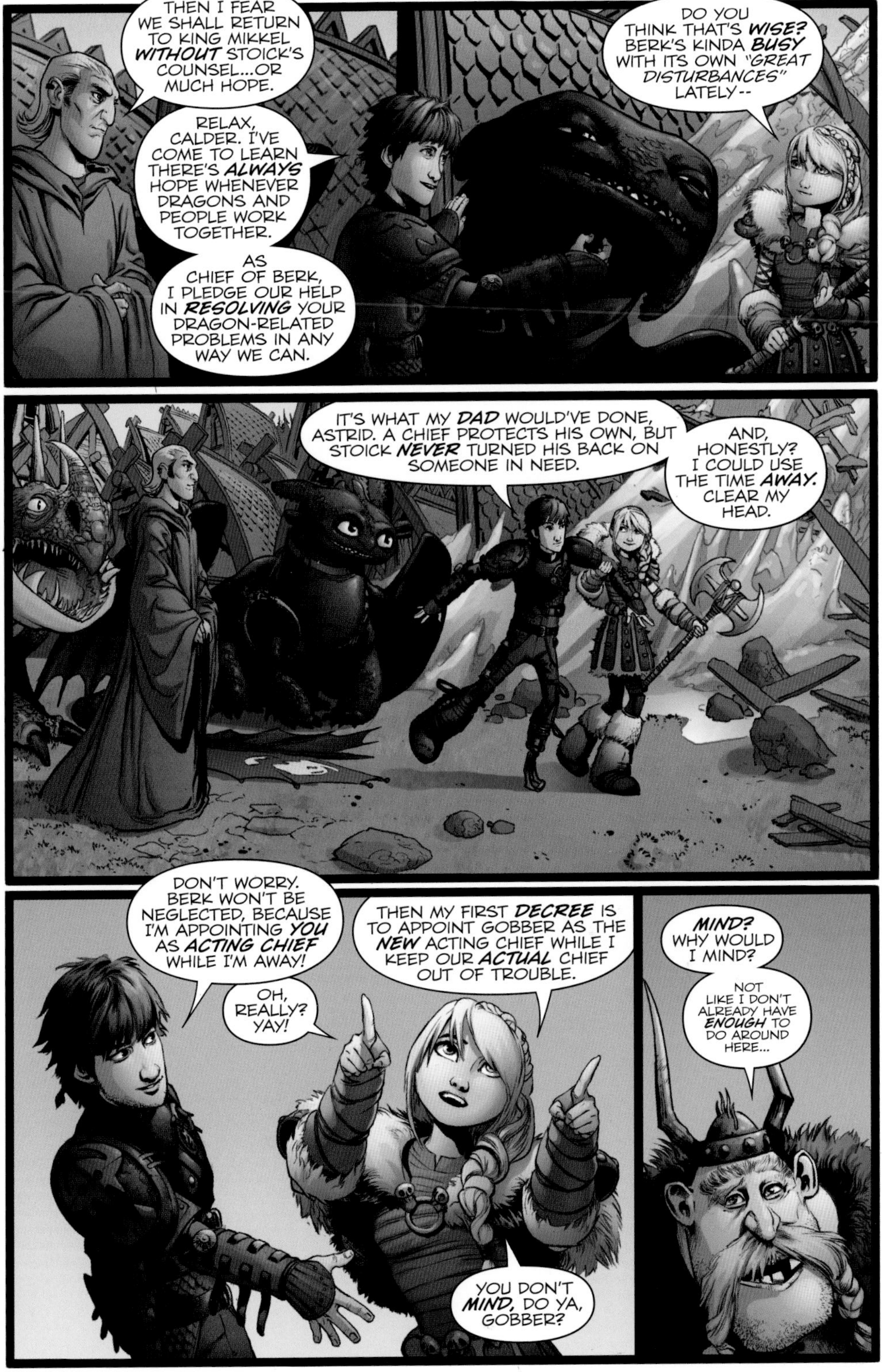
THEN I FEAR WE SHALL RETURN TO KING MIKKEL WITHOUT STOICK'S COUNSEL...OR MUCH HOPE.
RELAX, CALDER. I'VE COME TO LEARN THERE'S ALWAYS HOPE WHENEVER DRAGONS AND PEOPLE WORK TOGETHER.
AS CHIEF OF BERK, I PLEDGE OUR HELP IN RESOLVING YOUR DRAGON-RELATED PROBLEMS IN ANY WAY WE CAN.
DO YOU THINK THAT'S WISE? BERK'S KINDA BUSY WITH ITS OWN "GREAT DISTURBANCES" LATELY--
IT'S WHAT MY DAD WOULD'VE DONE, ASTRID. A CHIEF PROTECTS HIS OWN, BUT STOICK NEVER TURNED HIS BACK ON SOMEONE IN NEED.
AND, HONESTLY? I COULD USE THE TIME AWAY. CLEAR MY HEAD.
DON'T WORRY. BERK WON'T BE NEGLECTED, BECAUSE I'M APPOINTING YOU AS ACTING CHIEF WHILE I'M AWAY!
OH, REALLY? YAY!
THEN MY FIRST DECREE IS TO APPOINT GOBBER AS THE NEW ACTING CHIEF WHILE I KEEP OUR ACTUAL CHIEF OUT OF TROUBLE.
YOU DON'T MIND, DO YA, GOBBER?
MIND? WHY WOULD I MIND?
NOT LIKE I DON'T ALREADY HAVE ENOUGH TO DO AROUND HERE...

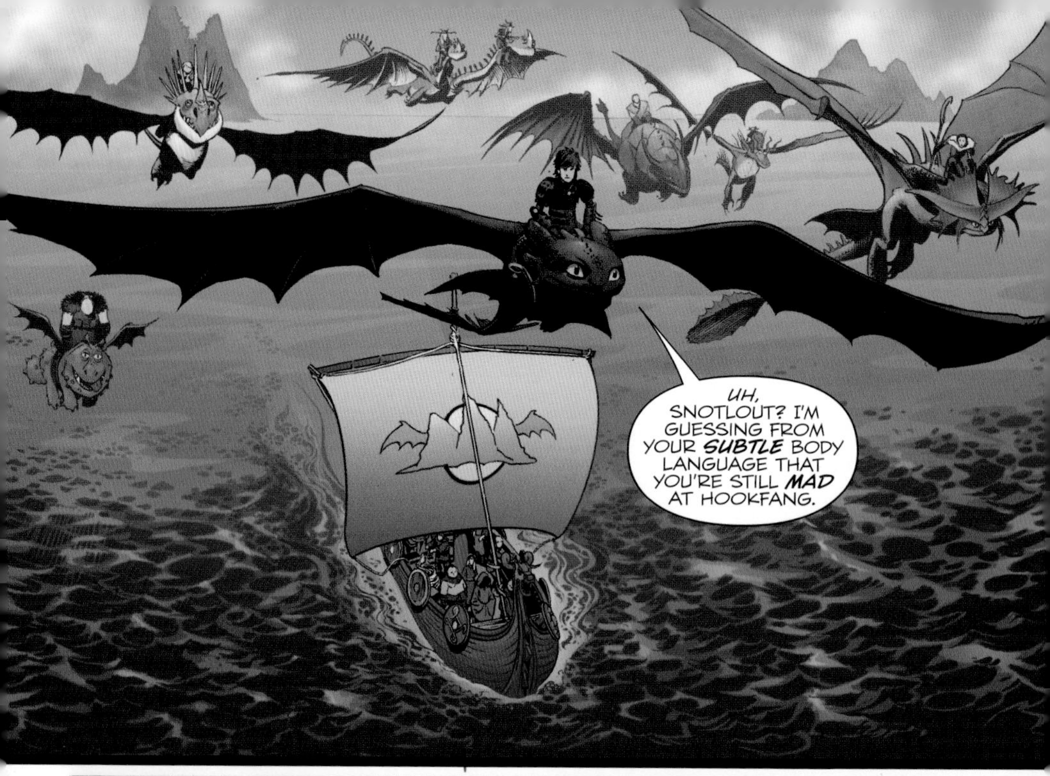
UH, SNOTLOUT? I'M GUESSING FROM YOUR SUBTLE BODY LANGUAGE THAT YOU'RE STILL MAD AT HOOKFANG.

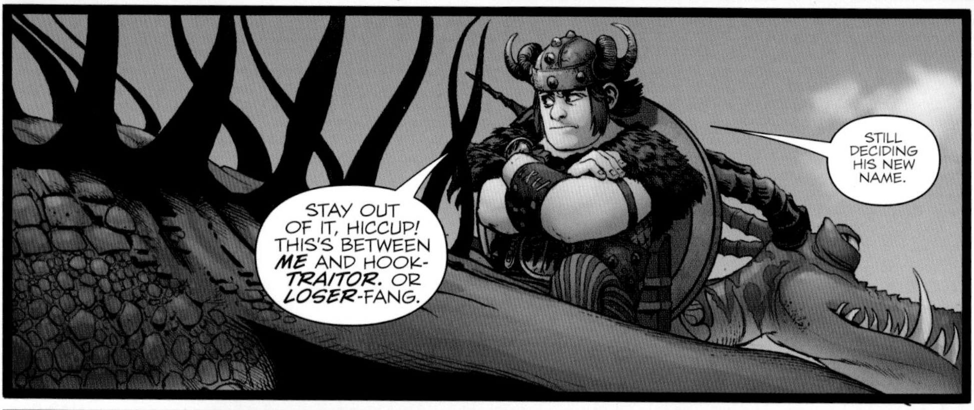
STAY OUT OF IT, HICCUP! THIS'S BETWEEN ME AND HOOK-TRAITOR. OR LOSER-FANG.
STILL DECIDING HIS NEW NAME.

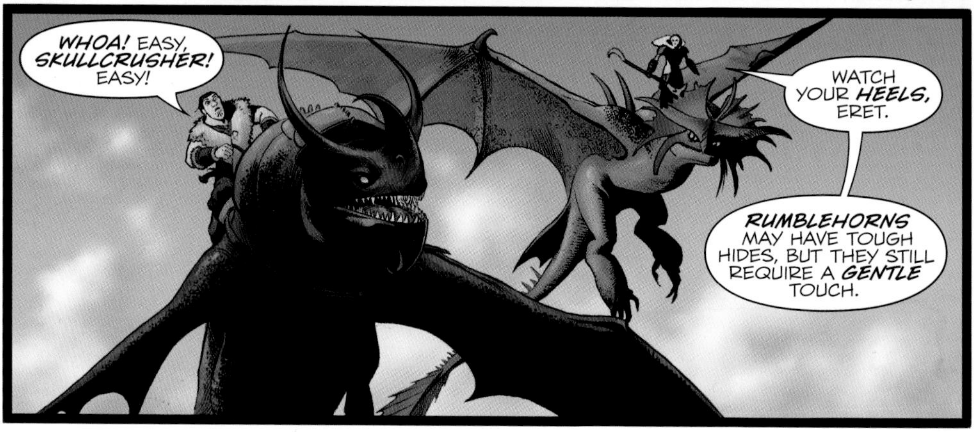
WHOA! EASY, SKULLCRUSHER! EASY!
WATCH YOUR HEELS, ERET.
RUMBLEHORNS MAY HAVE TOUGH HIDES, BUT THEY STILL REQUIRE A GENTLE TOUCH.

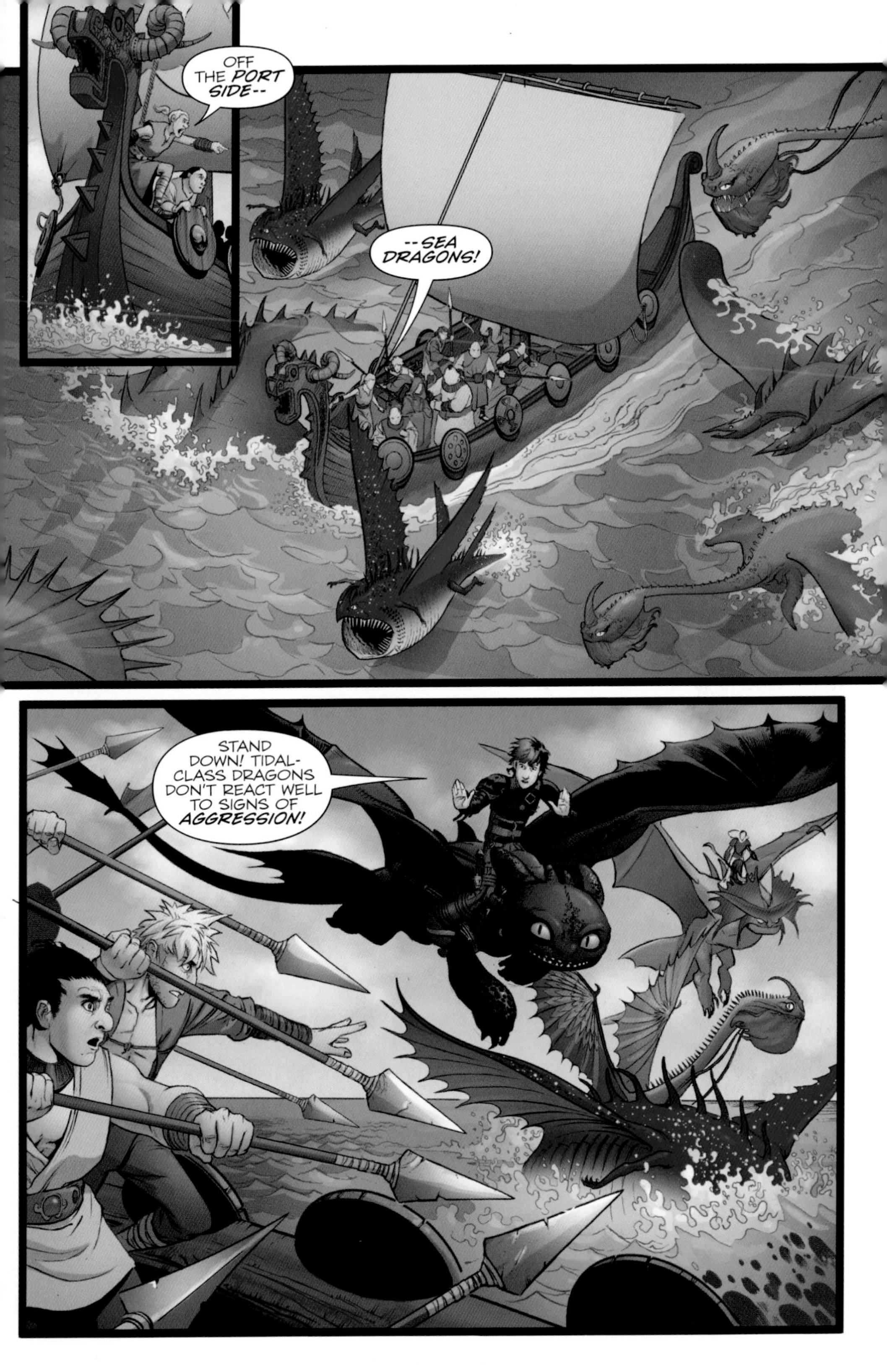

OFF THE PORT SIDE--
--SEA DRAGONS!
STAND DOWN! TIDAL-CLASS DRAGONS DON'T REACT WELL TO SIGNS OF AGGRESSION!

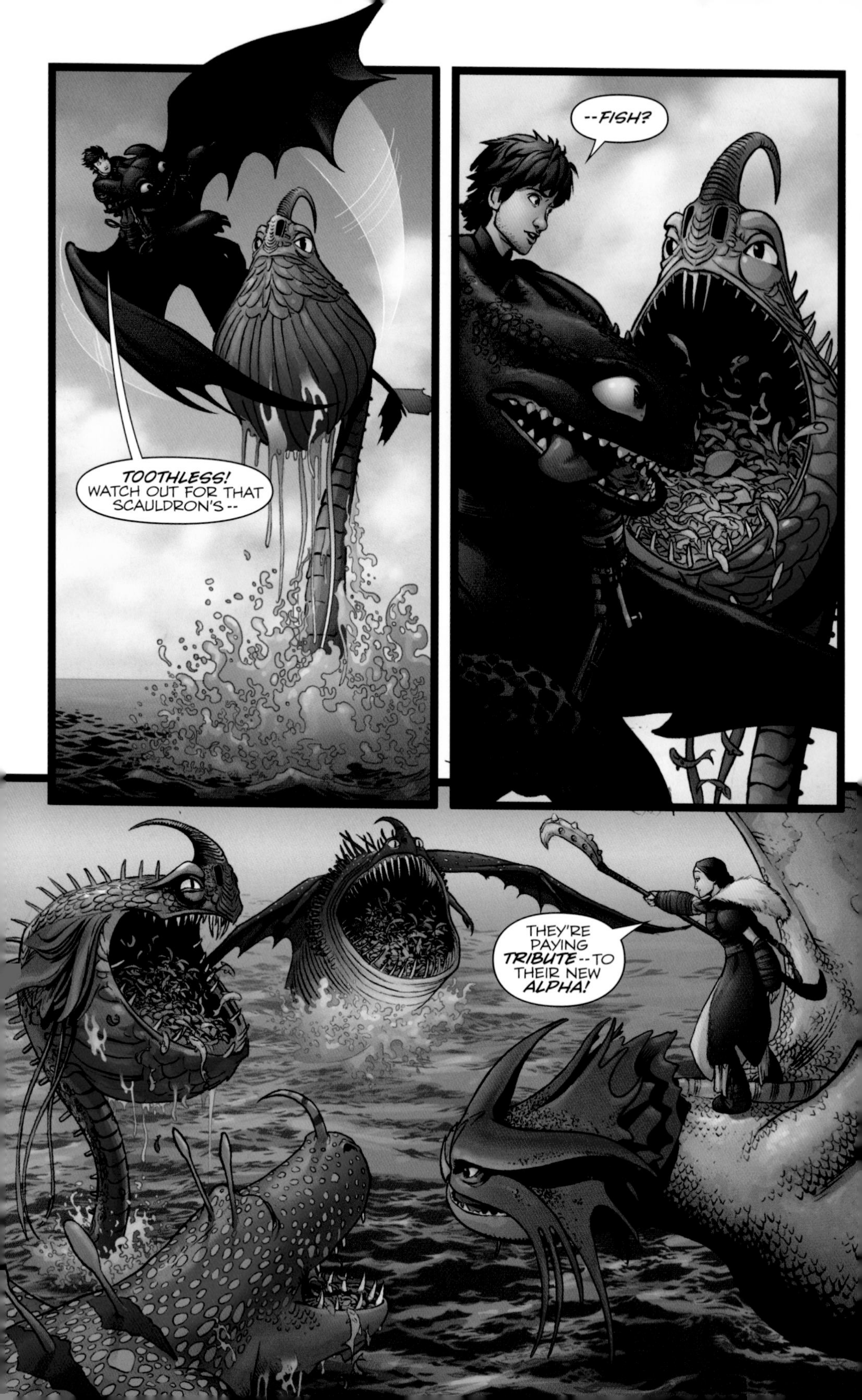
TOOTHLESS! WATCH OUT FOR THAT SCAULDRON'S --
--FISH?
THEY'RE PAYING TRIBUTE -- TO THEIR NEW ALPHA!

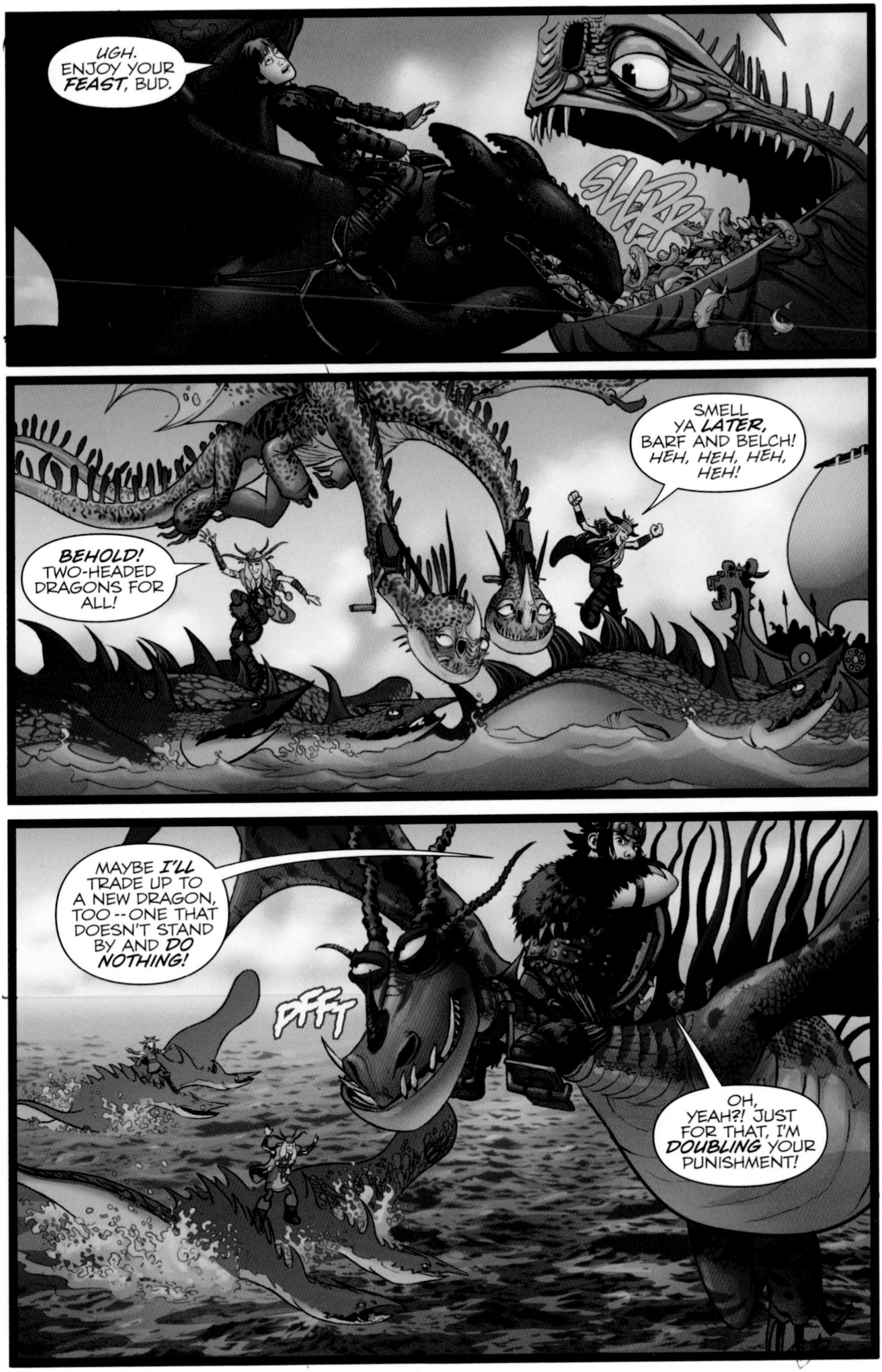
UGH. ENJOY YOUR FEAST, BUD.
SLURP
SMELL YA LATER, BARF AND BELCH! HEH, HEH, HEH, HEH!
BEHOLD! TWO-HEADED DRAGONS FOR ALL!
MAYBE I'LL TRADE UP TO A NEW DRAGON, TOO--ONE THAT DOESN'T STAND BY AND DO NOTHING!
PFFT
OH, YEAH?! JUST FOR THAT, I'M DOUBLING YOUR PUNISHMENT!

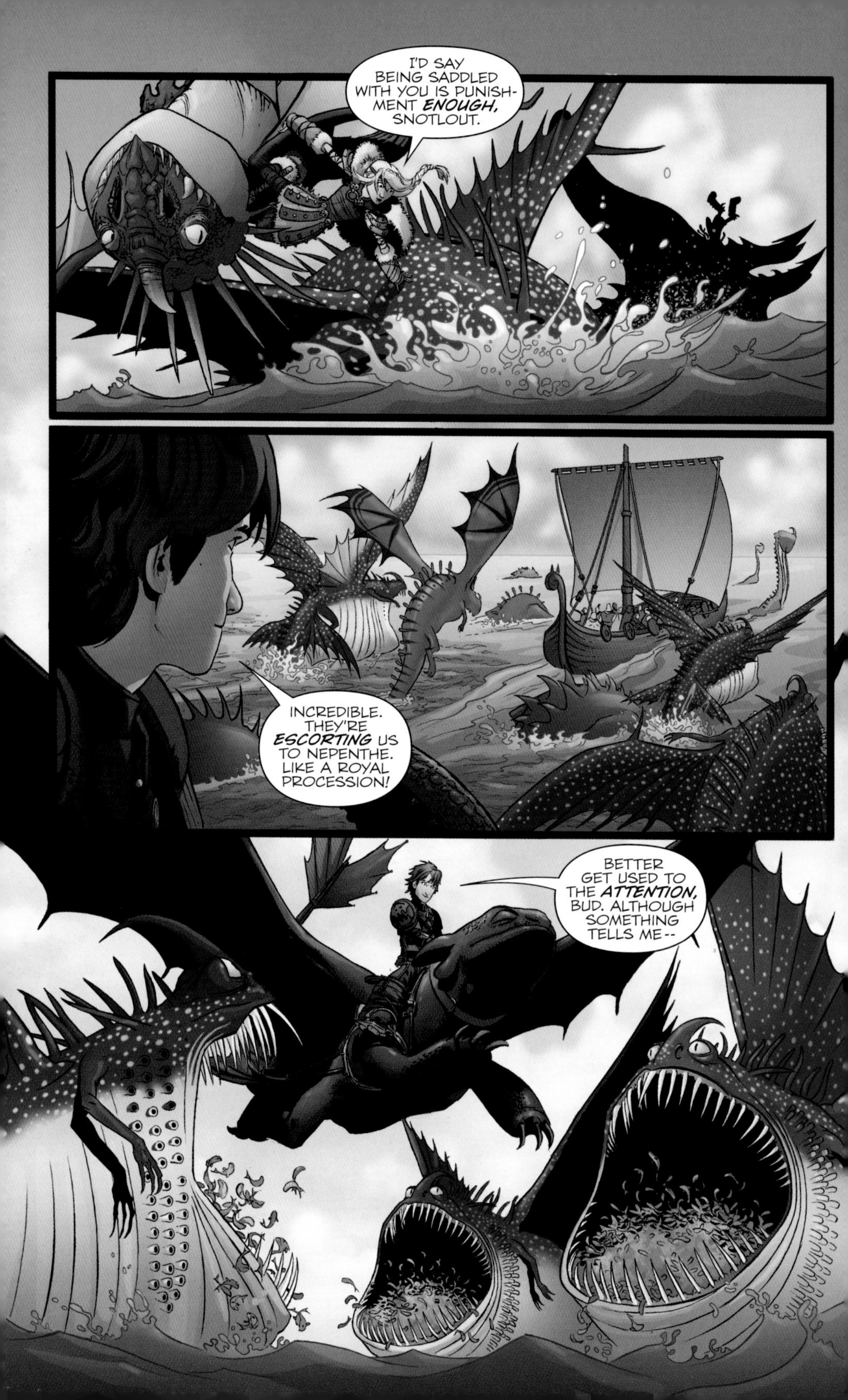
I'D SAY BEING SADDLED WITH YOU IS PUNISHMENT ENOUGH, SNOTLOUT.
INCREDIBLE. THEY'RE ESCORTING US TO NEPENTHE. LIKE A ROYAL PROCESSION!
BETTER GET USED TO THE ATTENTION, BUD. ALTHOUGH SOMETHING TELLS ME--

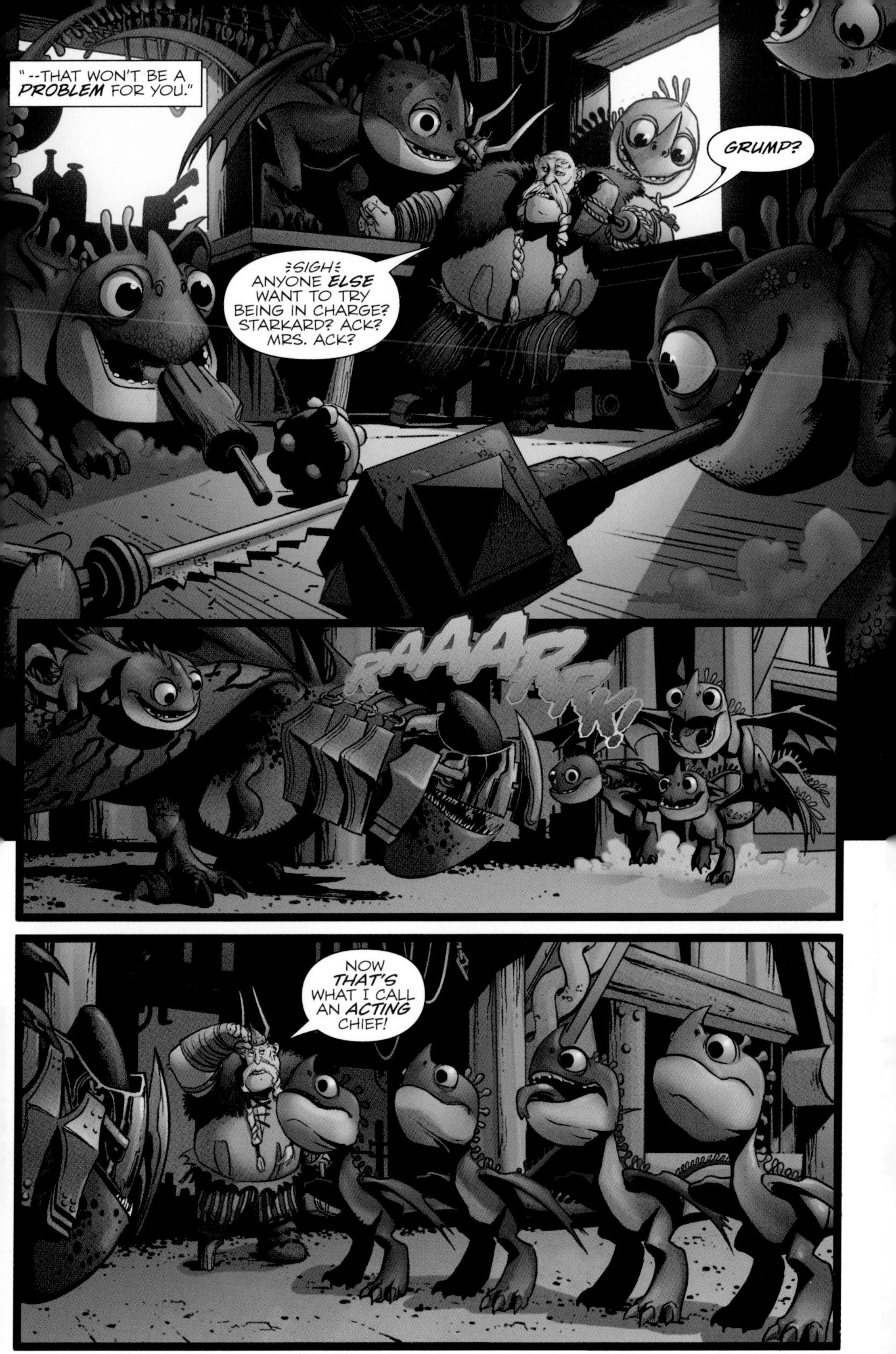
"--THAT WON'T BE A PROBLEM FOR YOU."
GRUMP?
=SIGH= ANYONE ELSE WANT TO TRY BEING IN CHARGE? STARKARD? ACK? MRS. ACK?
RAAARRW!
NOW THAT'S WHAT I CALL AN ACTING CHIEF!

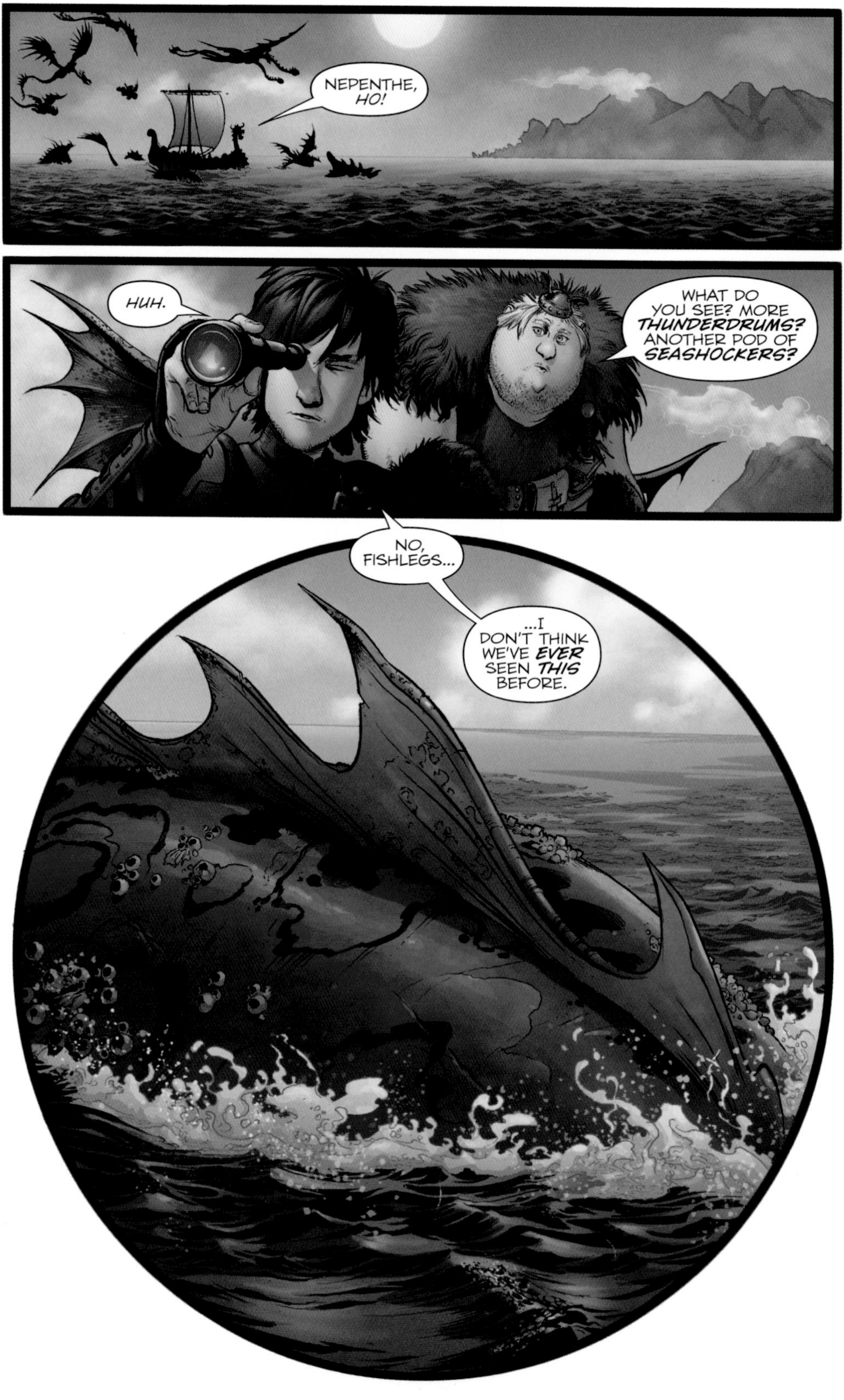
NEPENTHE, HO!
HUH.
WHAT DO YOU SEE? MORE THUNDERDRUMS? ANOTHER POD OF SEASHOCKERS?
NO, FISHLEGS...
...I DON'T THINK WE'VE EVER SEEN THIS BEFORE.

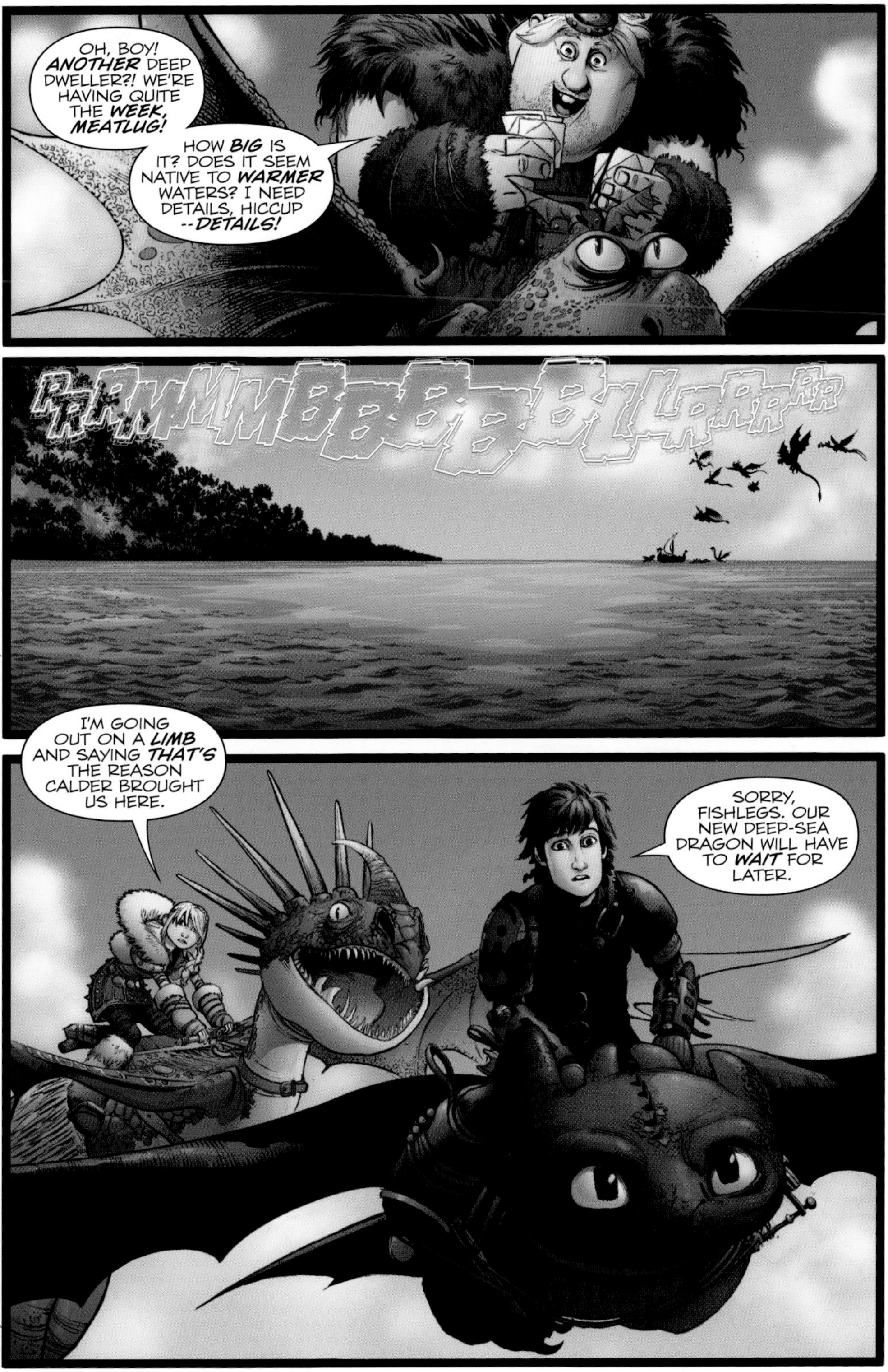
OH, BOY! ANOTHER DEEP DWELLER?! WE'RE HAVING QUITE THE WEEK, MEATLUG!
HOW BIG IS IT? DOES IT SEEM NATIVE TO WARMER WATERS? I NEED DETAILS, HICCUP --DETAILS!
PRRMMMBBB-B-BBLRRRRR
I'M GOING OUT ON A LIMB AND SAYING THAT'S THE REASON CALDER BROUGHT US HERE.
SORRY, FISHLEGS. OUR NEW DEEP-SEA DRAGON WILL HAVE TO WAIT FOR LATER.

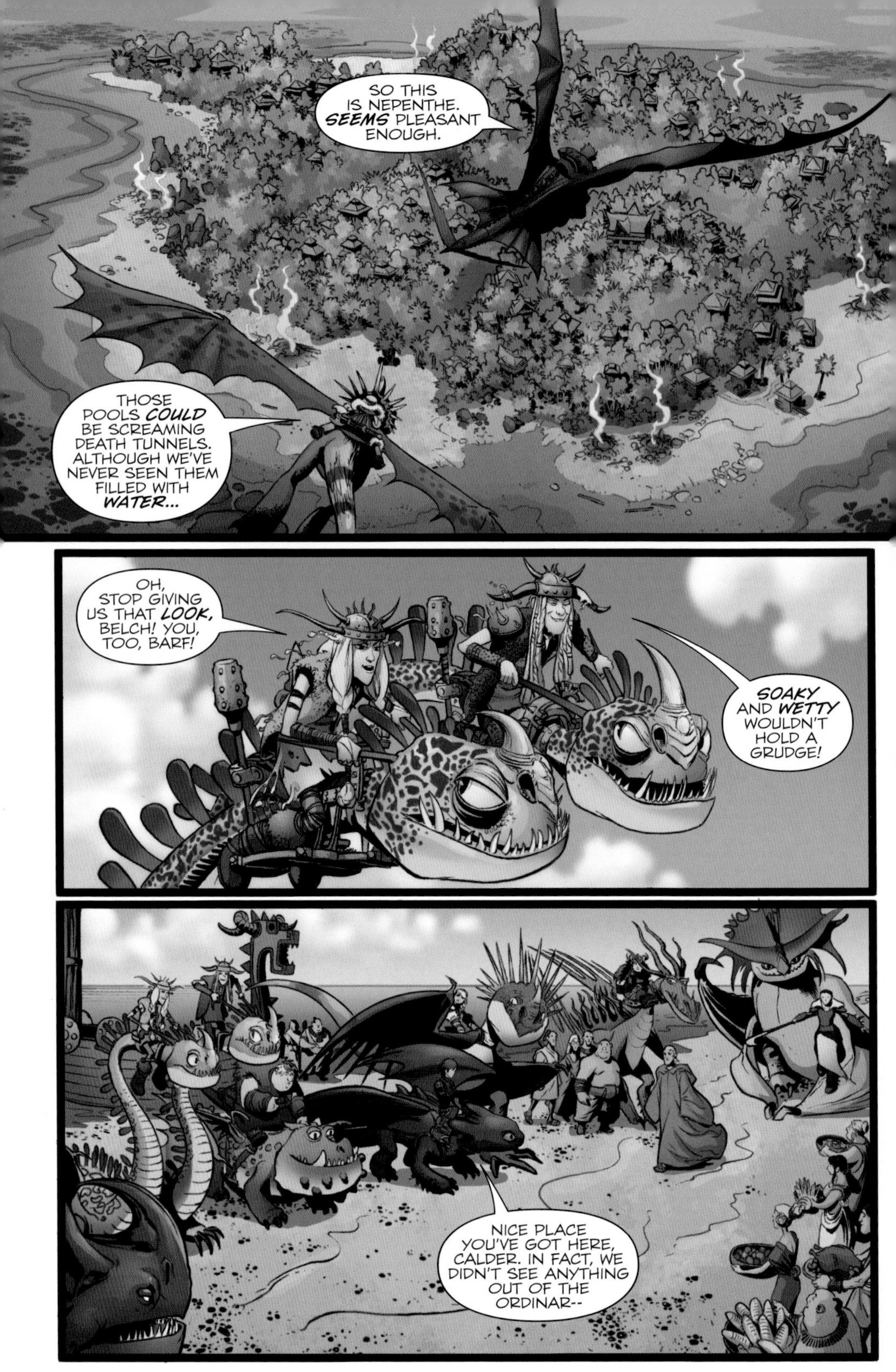
SO THIS IS NEPENTHE. SEEMS PLEASANT ENOUGH.
THOSE POOLS COULD BE SCREAMING DEATH TUNNELS. ALTHOUGH WE'VE NEVER SEEN THEM FILLED WITH WATER...
OH, STOP GIVING US THAT LOOK, BELCH! YOU, TOO, BARF!
SOAKY AND WETTY WOULDN'T HOLD A GRUDGE!
NICE PLACE YOU'VE GOT HERE, CALDER. IN FACT, WE DIDN'T SEE ANYTHING OUT OF THE ORDINAR--

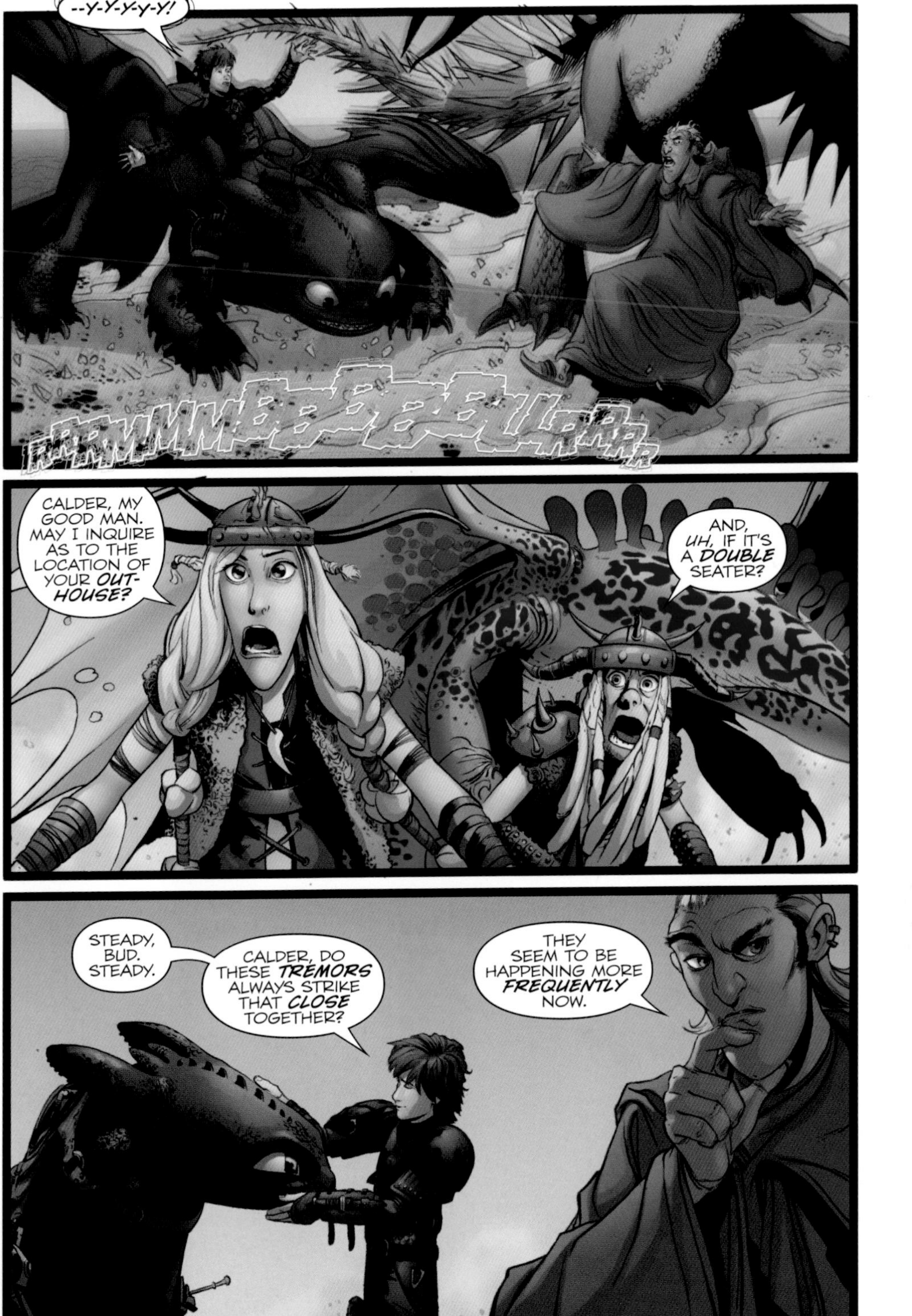
--Y-Y-Y-Y-Y!
CALDER, MY GOOD MAN. MAY I INQUIRE AS TO THE LOCATION OF YOUR OUT-HOUSE?
AND, UH, IF IT'S A DOUBLE SEATER?
STEADY, BUD. STEADY.
CALDER, DO THESE TREMORS ALWAYS STRIKE THAT CLOSE TOGETHER?
THEY SEEM TO BE HAPPENING MORE FREQUENTLY NOW.

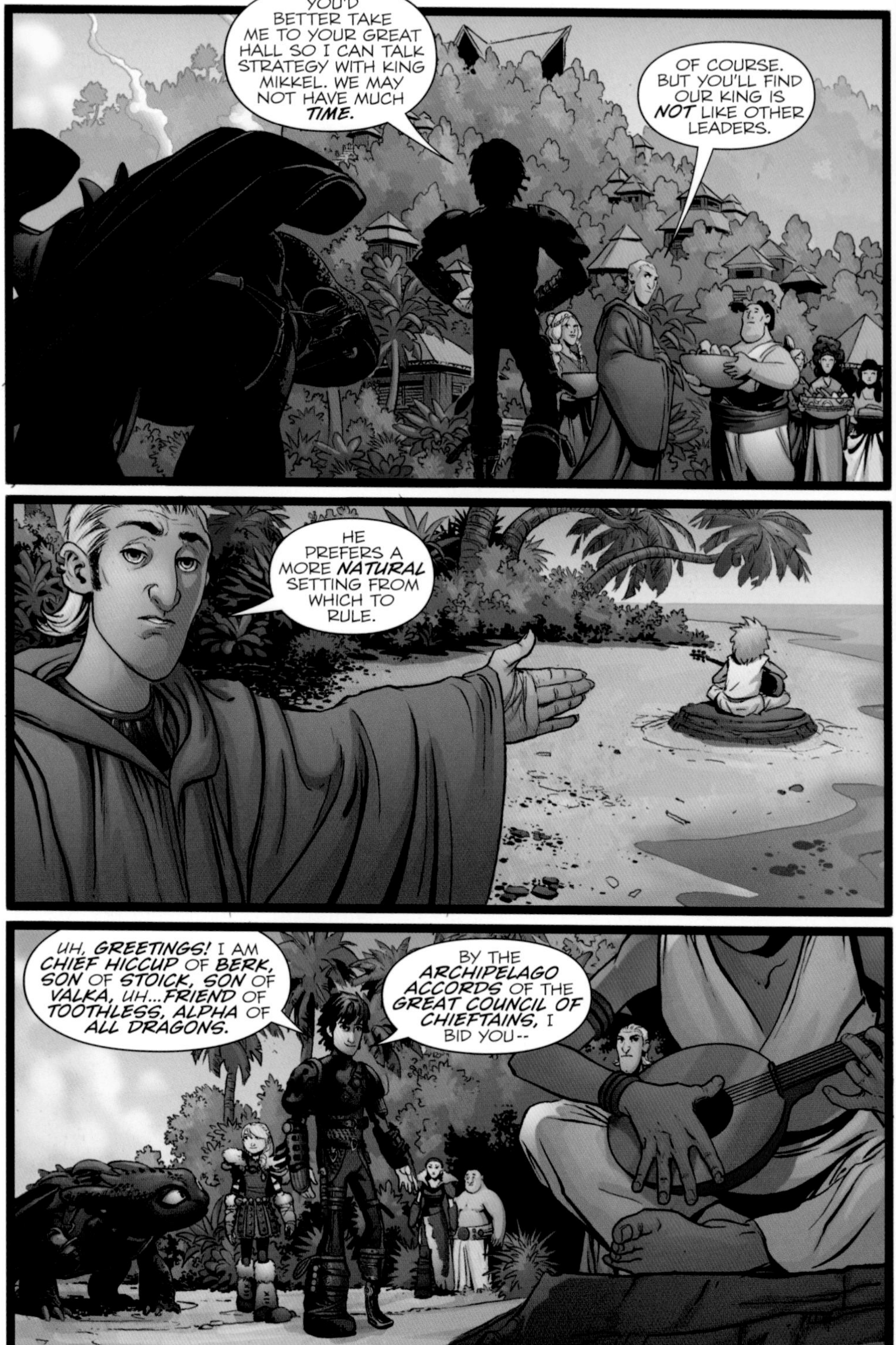
YOU'D BETTER TAKE ME TO YOUR GREAT HALL SO I CAN TALK STRATEGY WITH KING MIKKEL. WE MAY NOT HAVE MUCH TIME.
OF COURSE. BUT YOU'LL FIND OUR KING IS NOT LIKE OTHER LEADERS.
HE PREFERS A MORE NATURAL SETTING FROM WHICH TO RULE.
UH, GREETINGS! I AM CHIEF HICCUP OF BERK, SON OF STOICK, SON OF VALKA, UH...FRIEND OF TOOTHLESS, ALPHA OF ALL DRAGONS.
BY THE ARCHIPELAGO ACCORDS OF THE GREAT COUNCIL OF CHIEFTAINS, I BID YOU--

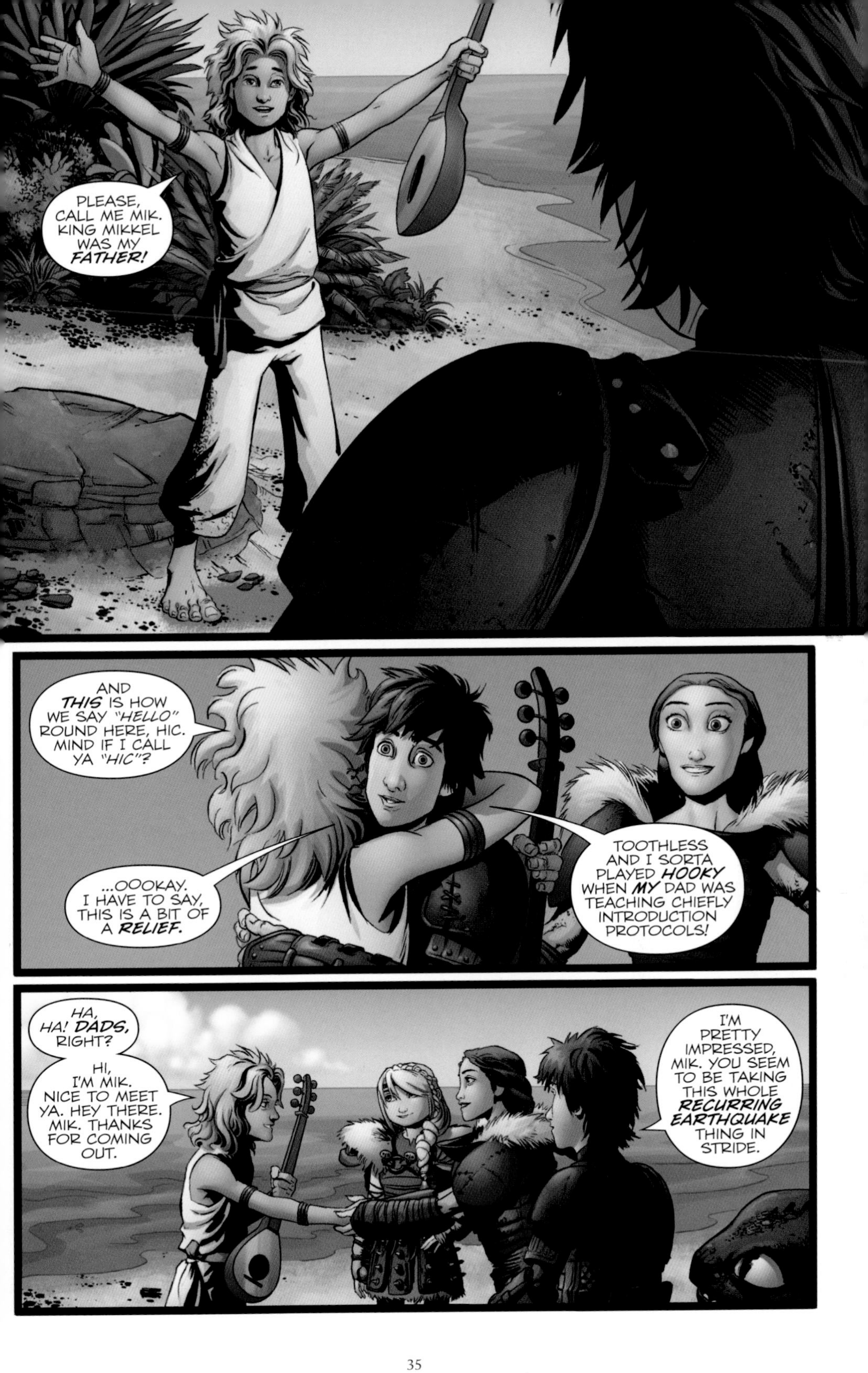
PLEASE, CALL ME MIK. KING MIKKEL WAS MY FATHER!
AND THIS IS HOW WE SAY "HELLO" ROUND HERE, HIC. MIND IF I CALL YA "HIC"?
...OOOKAY. I HAVE TO SAY, THIS IS A BIT OF A RELIEF.
TOOTHLESS AND I SORTA PLAYED HOOKY WHEN MY DAD WAS TEACHING CHIEFLY INTRODUCTION PROTOCOLS!
HA, HA! DADS, RIGHT?
HI, I'M MIK. NICE TO MEET YA. HEY THERE. MIK. THANKS FOR COMING OUT.
I'M PRETTY IMPRESSED, MIK. YOU SEEM TO BE TAKING THIS WHOLE RECURRING EARTHQUAKE THING IN STRIDE.

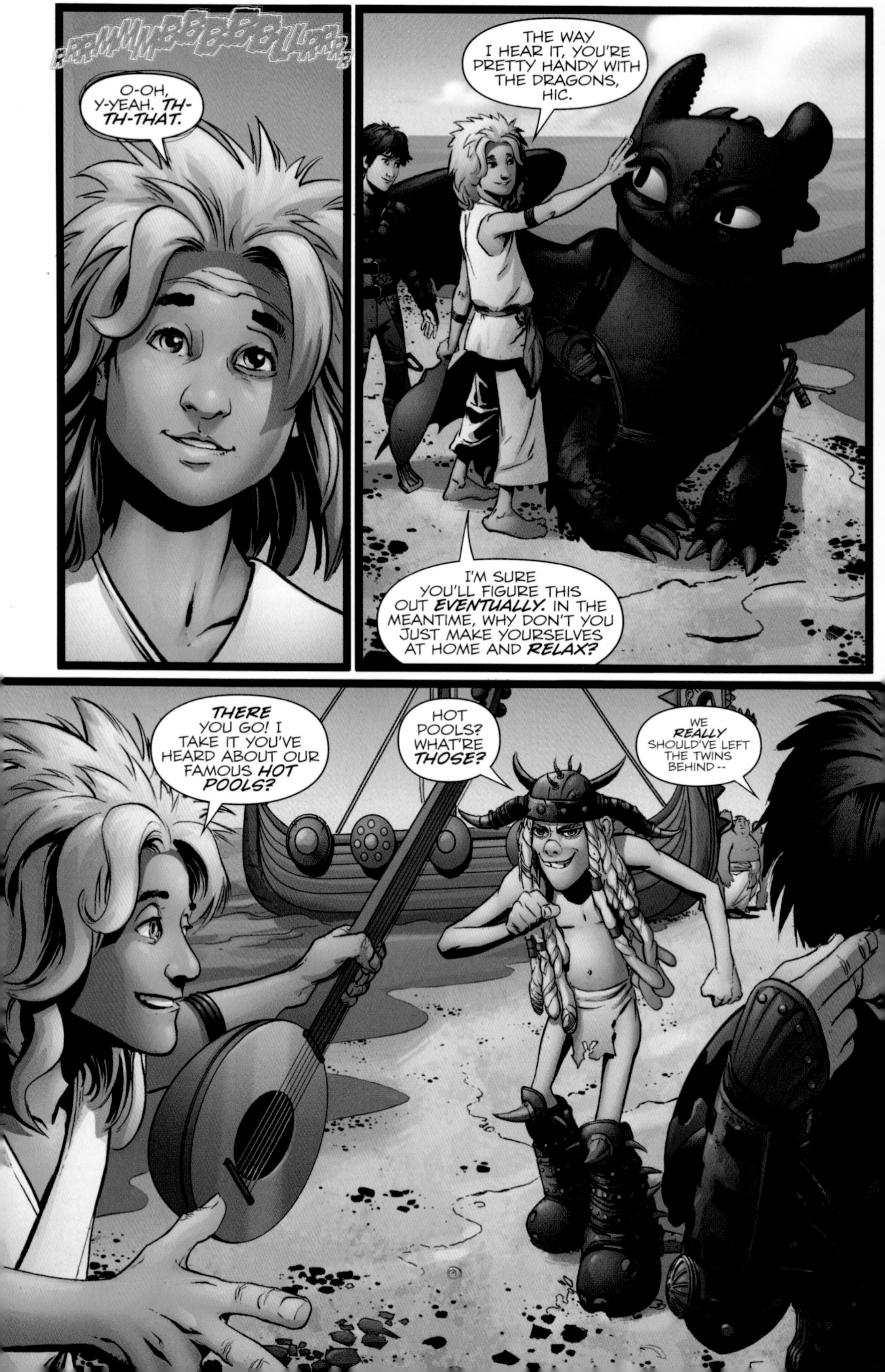
O-OH, Y-YEAH. *TH-TH-THAT.*
THE WAY I HEAR IT, YOU'RE PRETTY HANDY WITH THE DRAGONS, HIC.
I'M SURE YOU'LL FIGURE THIS OUT ***EVENTUALLY.*** IN THE MEANTIME, WHY DON'T YOU JUST MAKE YOURSELVES AT HOME AND ***RELAX?***
THERE YOU GO! I TAKE IT YOU'VE HEARD ABOUT OUR FAMOUS ***HOT POOLS?***
HOT POOLS? WHAT'RE ***THOSE?***
WE ***REALLY*** SHOULD'VE LEFT THE TWINS BEHIND --

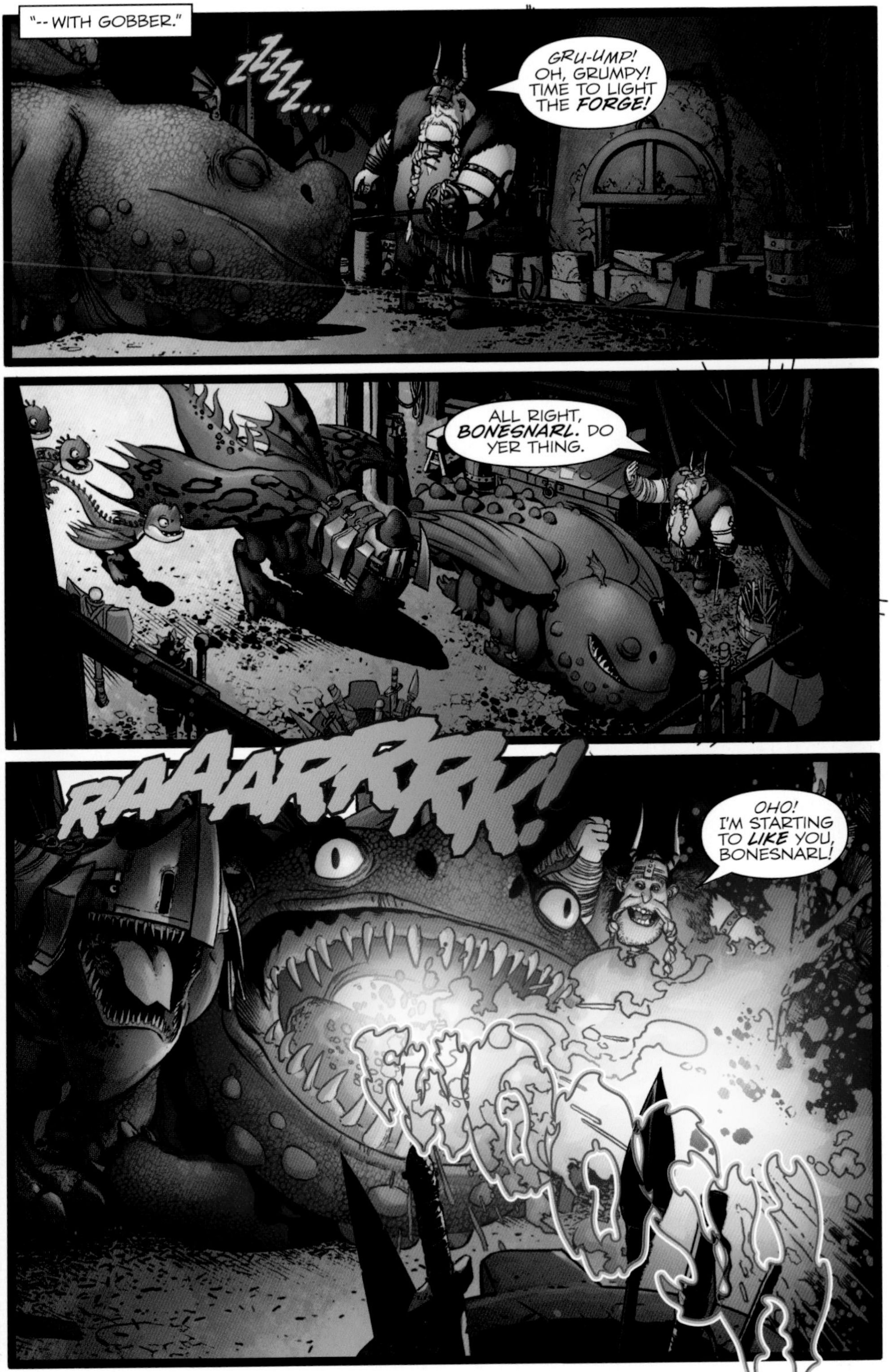
"-- WITH GOBBER."
GRU-UMP! OH, GRUMPY! TIME TO LIGHT THE FORGE!
ALL RIGHT, BONESNARL. DO YER THING.
OHO! I'M STARTING TO LIKE YOU, BONESNARL!

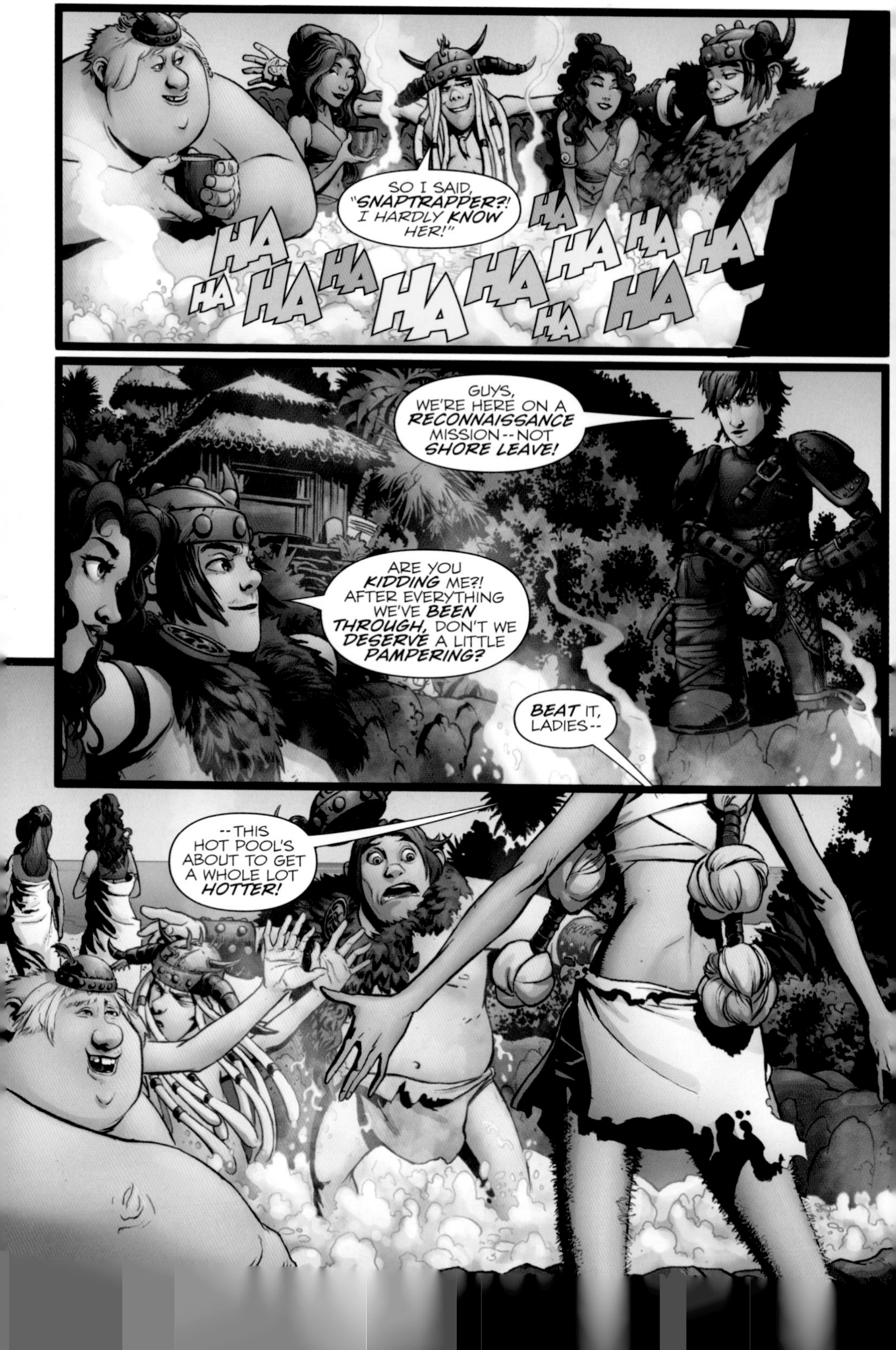
SO I SAID, "SNAPTRAPPER?! I HARDLY KNOW HER!"
HA HA HA HA HA HA HA HA HA HA HA HA HA
GUYS, WE'RE HERE ON A RECONNAISSANCE MISSION--NOT SHORE LEAVE!
ARE YOU KIDDING ME?! AFTER EVERYTHING WE'VE BEEN THROUGH, DON'T WE DESERVE A LITTLE PAMPERING?
BEAT IT, LADIES--
--THIS HOT POOL'S ABOUT TO GET A WHOLE LOT HOTTER!

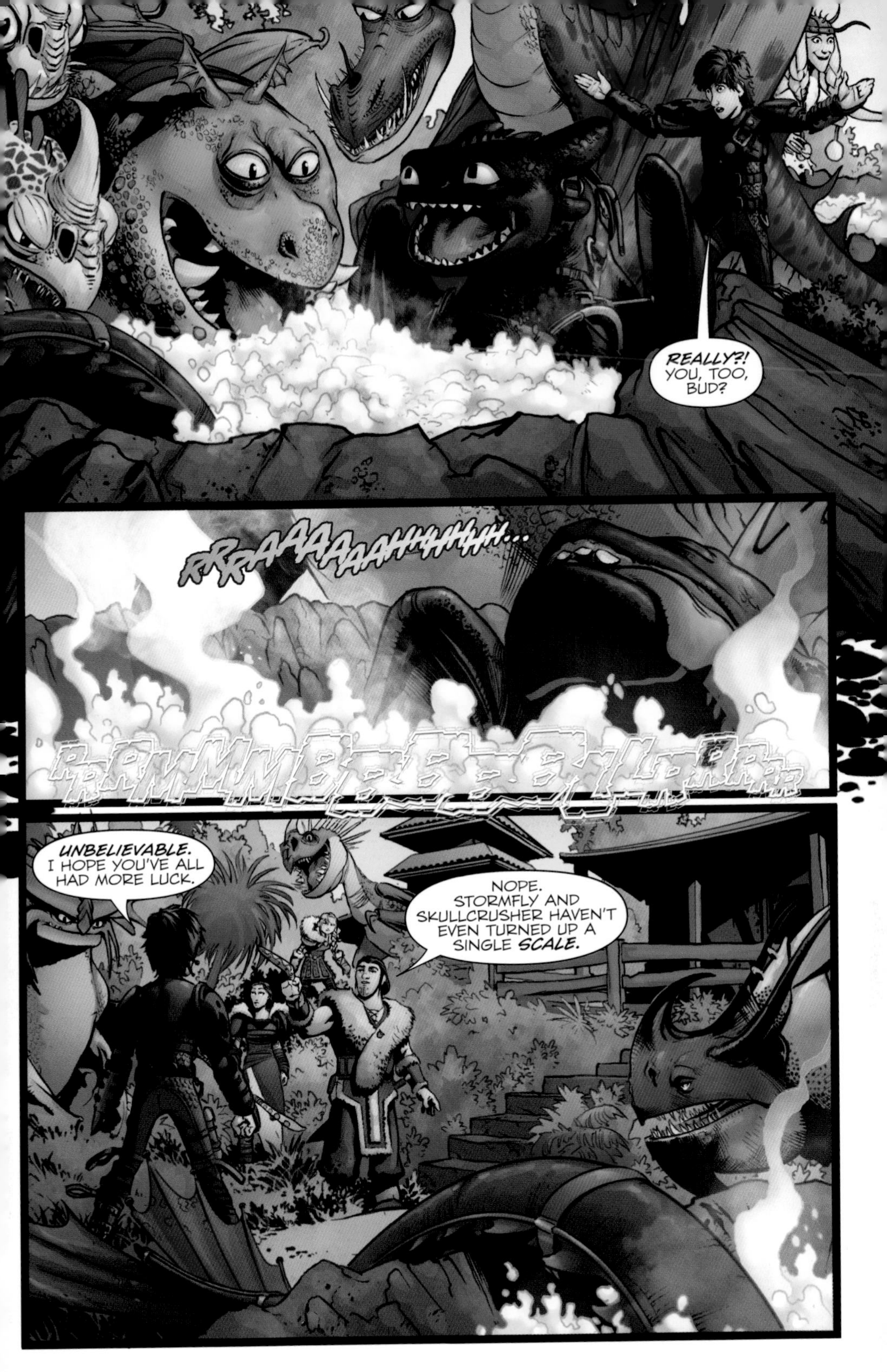
REALLY?! YOU, TOO, BUD?
RRRAAAAAAAHHHHHH...
RRRMMMBLE BLE BLE RRRRR
UNBELIEVABLE. I HOPE YOU'VE ALL HAD MORE LUCK.
NOPE. STORMFLY AND SKULLCRUSHER HAVEN'T EVEN TURNED UP A SINGLE SCALE.

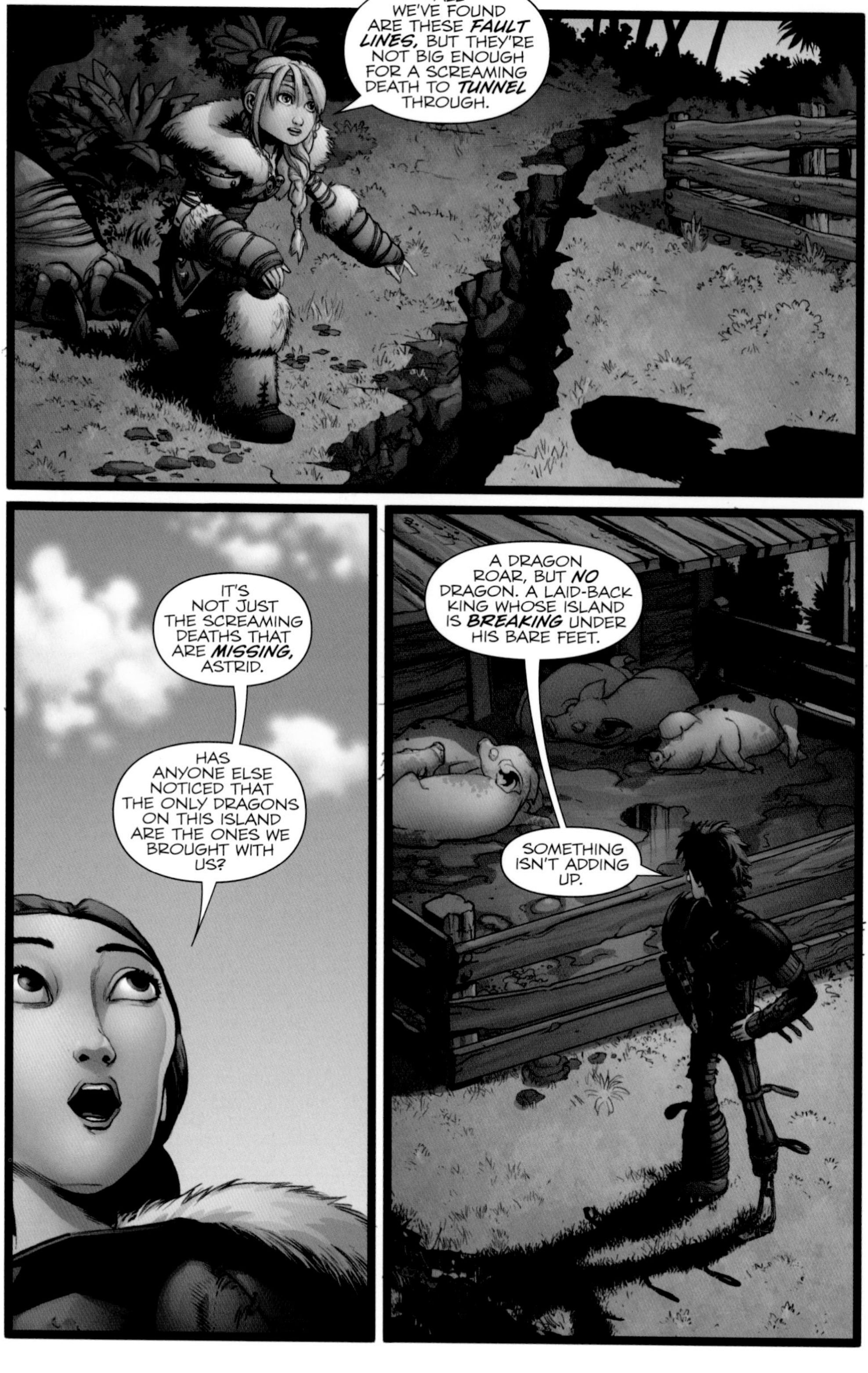
ALL WE'VE FOUND ARE THESE *FAULT LINES,* BUT THEY'RE NOT BIG ENOUGH FOR A SCREAMING DEATH TO *TUNNEL* THROUGH.
IT'S NOT JUST THE SCREAMING DEATHS THAT ARE *MISSING,* ASTRID.
HAS ANYONE ELSE NOTICED THAT THE ONLY DRAGONS ON THIS ISLAND ARE THE ONES WE BROUGHT WITH US?
A DRAGON ROAR, BUT *NO* DRAGON. A LAID-BACK KING WHOSE ISLAND IS *BREAKING* UNDER HIS BARE FEET.
SOMETHING ISN'T ADDING UP.

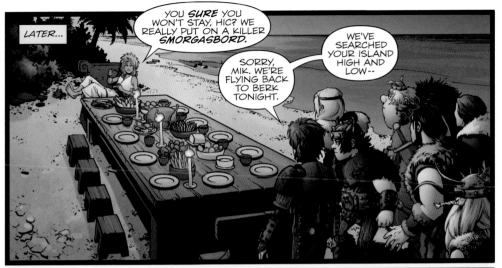

LATER...

YOU **SURE** YOU WON'T STAY, HIC? WE REALLY PUT ON A KILLER **SMORGASBORD.**

SORRY, MIK. WE'RE FLYING BACK TO BERK TONIGHT.

WE'VE SEARCHED YOUR ISLAND HIGH AND LOW--

--BUT WE COULDN'T FIND THE **SOURCE** OF YOUR TREMORS, DRAGON OR OTHERWISE.

SMEK

CHOMMP!

CRUNCH!

OM NOM!

SO IT JUST DOESN'T SEEM **RIGHT** FOR US TO ACCEPT ANY MORE OF YOUR...UH, HOSPITALITY...

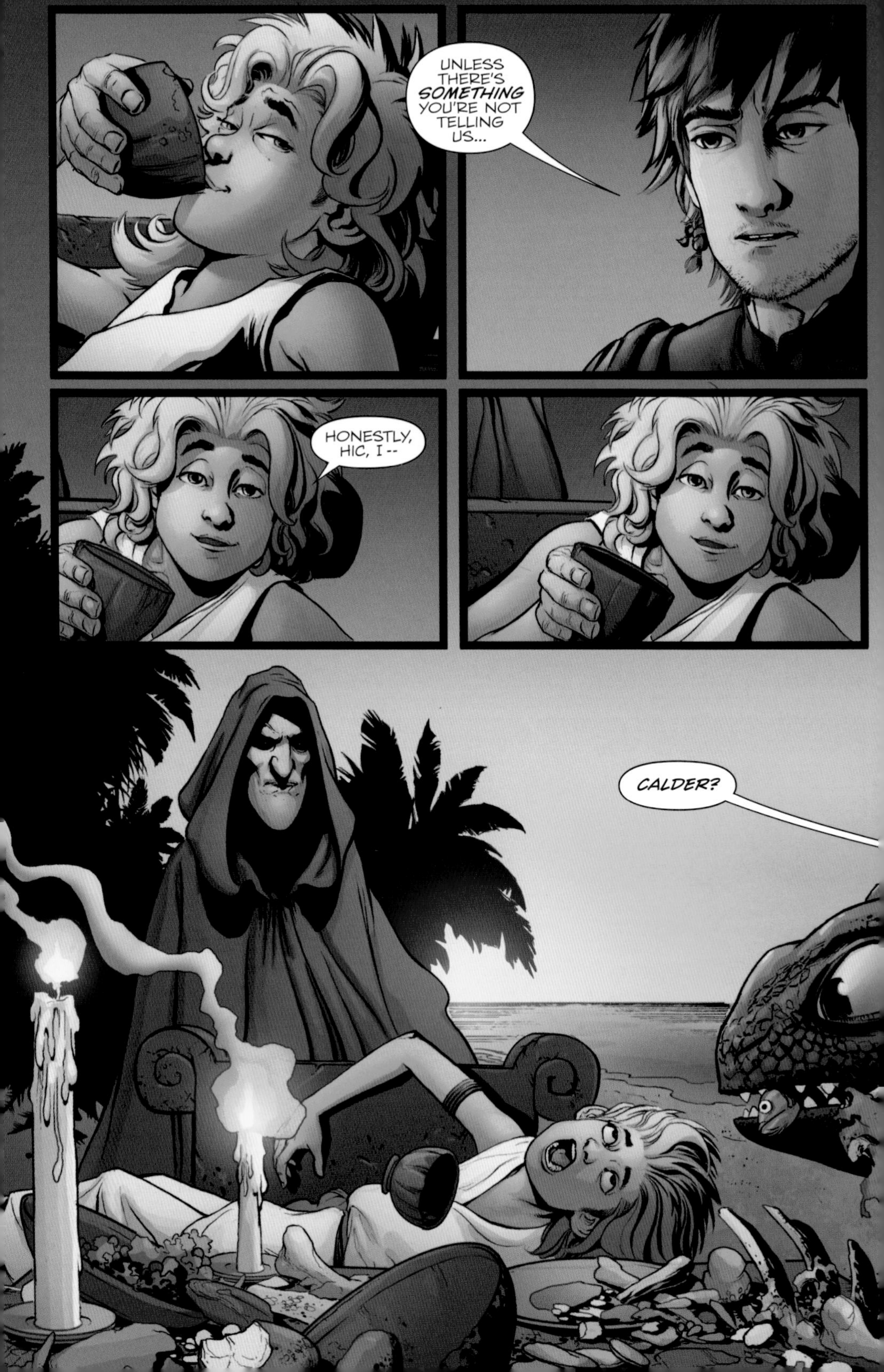
UNLESS THERE'S SOMETHING YOU'RE NOT TELLING US...
HONESTLY, HIC, I --
CALDER?

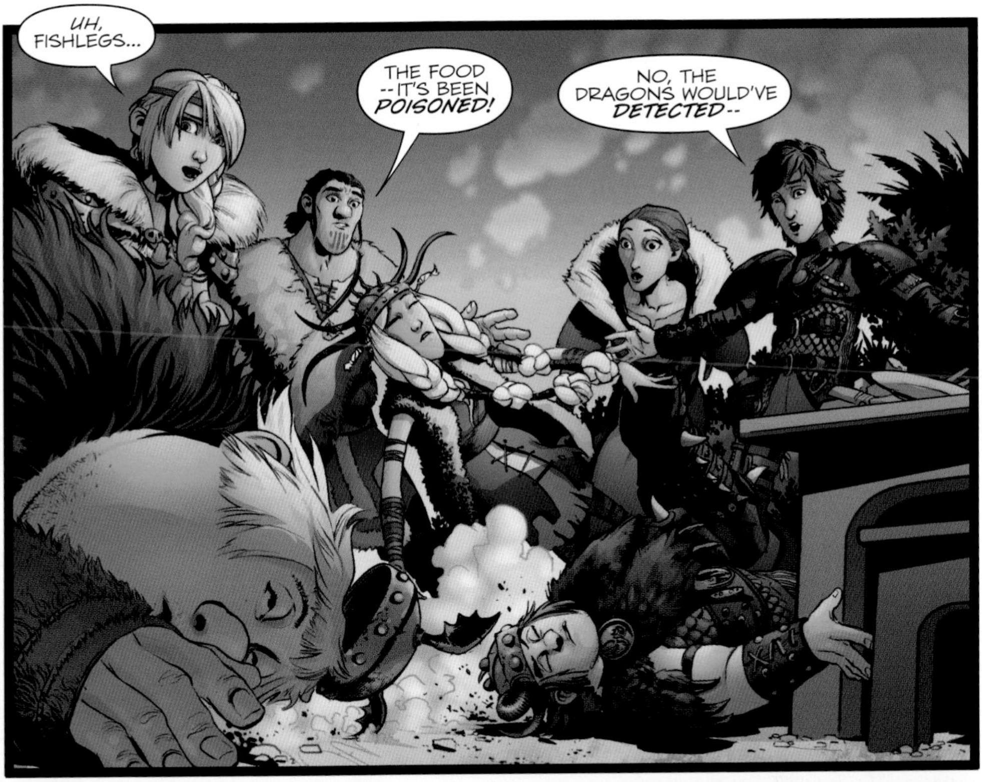
UH, FISHLEGS...
THE FOOD --IT'S BEEN POISONED!
NO, THE DRAGONS WOULD'VE DETECTED--

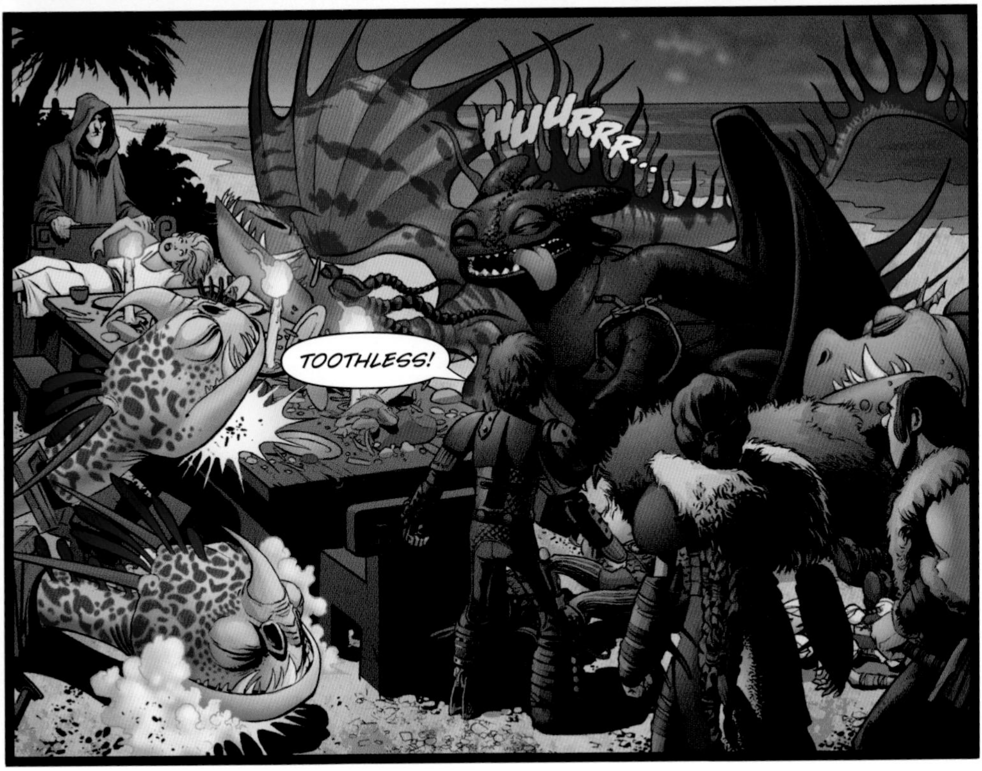
HUURRR...
TOOTHLESS!

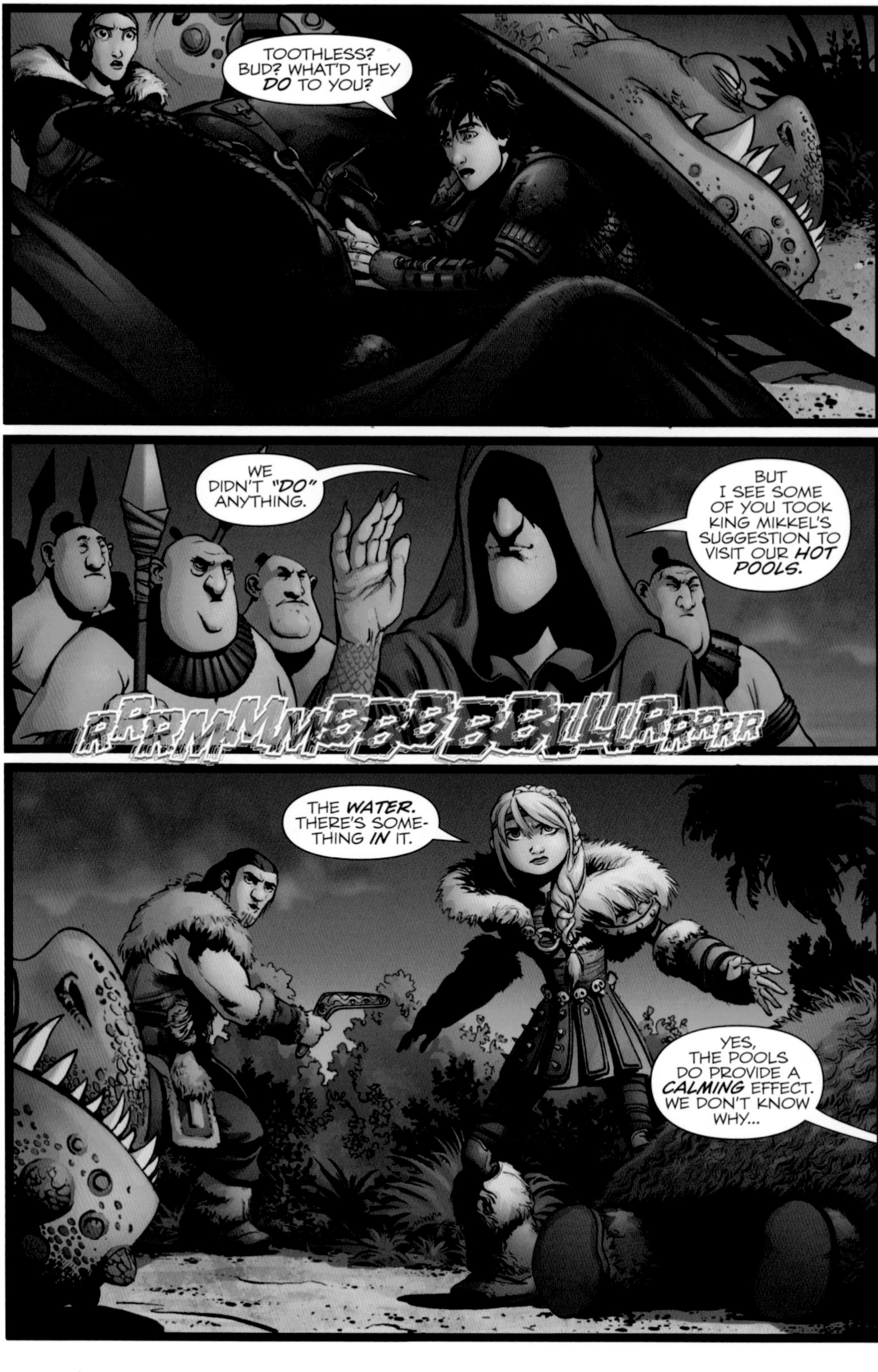
TOOTHLESS? BUD? WHAT'D THEY *DO* TO YOU?
WE DIDN'T *"DO"* ANYTHING.
BUT I SEE SOME OF YOU TOOK KING MIKKEL'S SUGGESTION TO VISIT OUR ***HOT POOLS.***
rRRRMMMMBBBBBBLLURRRRRR
THE ***WATER.*** THERE'S SOME-THING ***IN*** IT.
YES, THE POOLS DO PROVIDE A ***CALMING*** EFFECT. WE DON'T KNOW WHY...

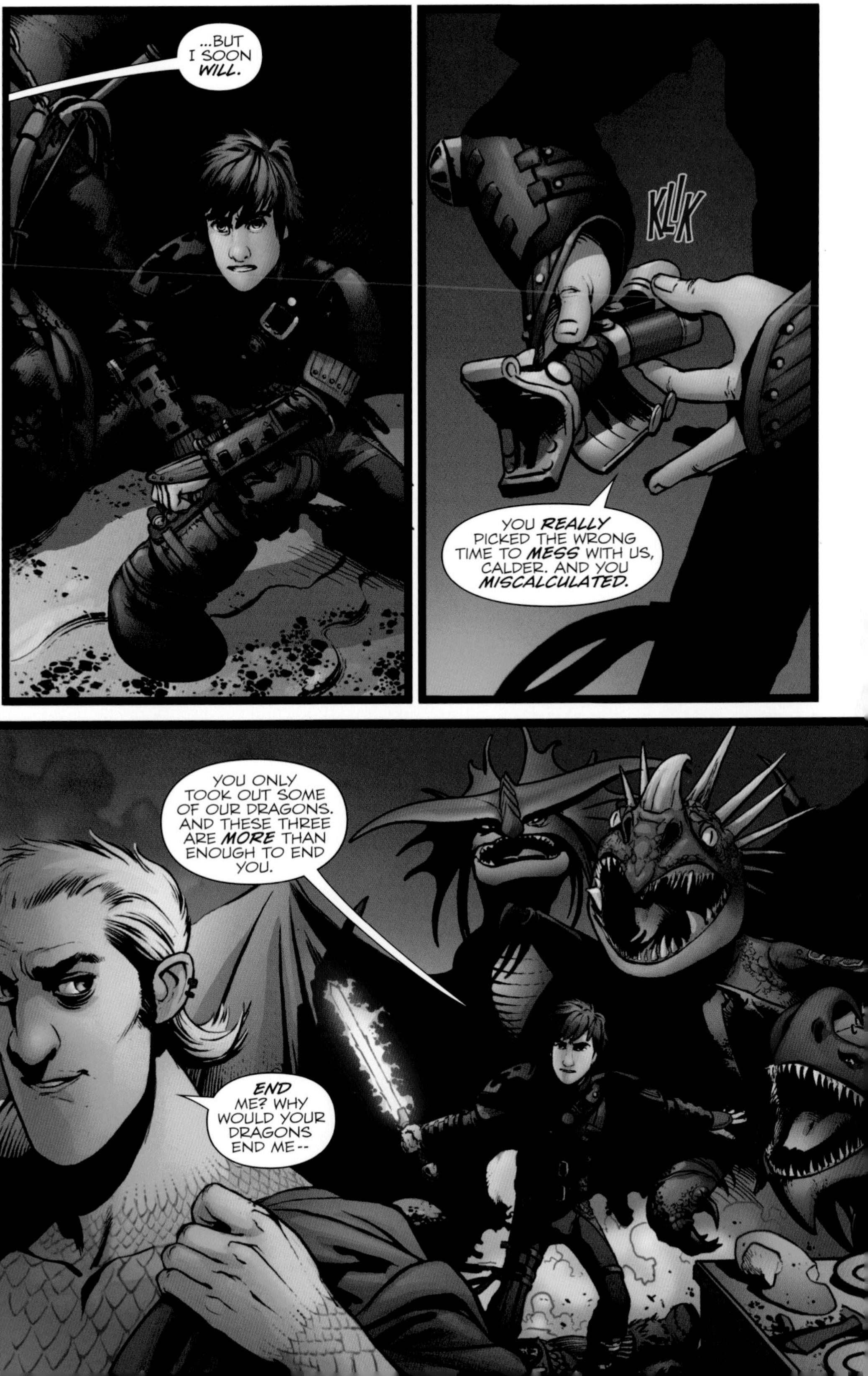
...BUT I SOON WILL.
KLIK
YOU REALLY PICKED THE WRONG TIME TO MESS WITH US, CALDER. AND YOU MISCALCULATED.
YOU ONLY TOOK OUT SOME OF OUR DRAGONS. AND THESE THREE ARE MORE THAN ENOUGH TO END YOU.
END ME? WHY WOULD YOUR DRAGONS END ME--

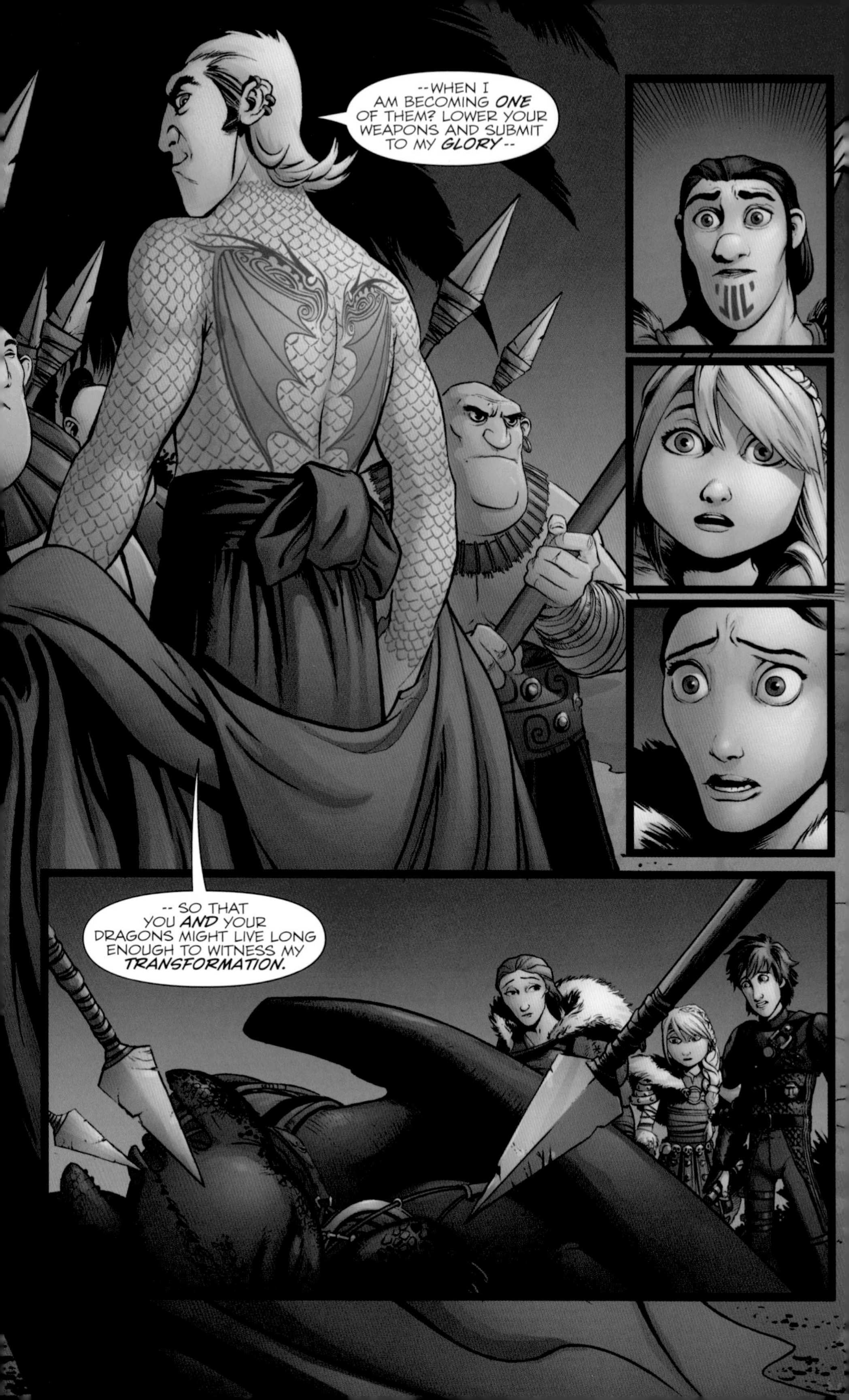
--WHEN I AM BECOMING ***ONE*** OF THEM? LOWER YOUR WEAPONS AND SUBMIT TO MY ***GLORY***--
-- SO THAT YOU ***AND*** YOUR DRAGONS MIGHT LIVE LONG ENOUGH TO WITNESS MY ***TRANSFORMATION.***

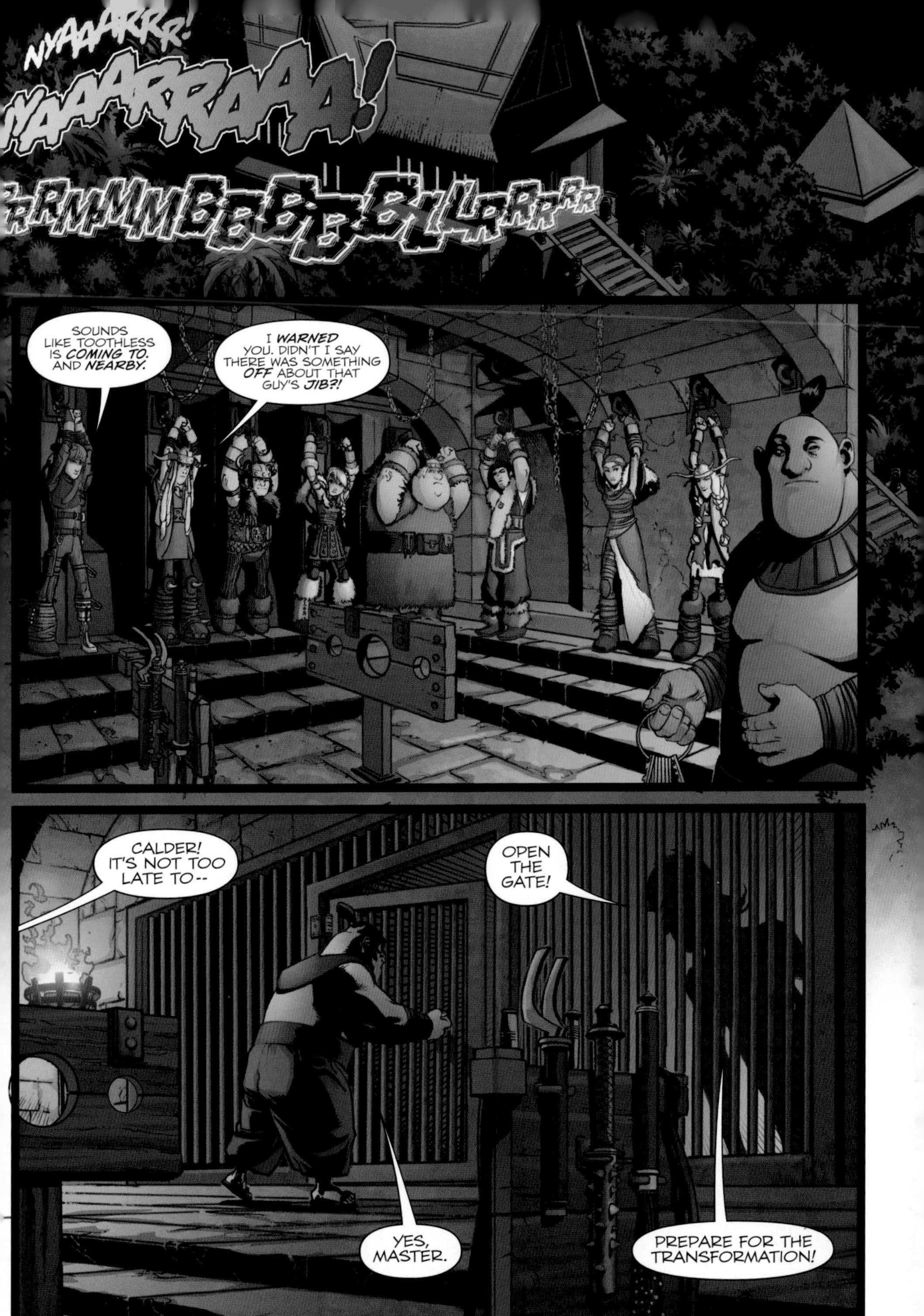
NYAAARRR!
NYAARRAAA!
SOUNDS LIKE TOOTHLESS IS COMING TO. AND NEARBY.
I WARNED YOU. DIDN'T I SAY THERE WAS SOMETHING OFF ABOUT THAT GUY'S JIB?!
CALDER! IT'S NOT TOO LATE TO--
OPEN THE GATE!
YES, MASTER.
PREPARE FOR THE TRANSFORMATION!

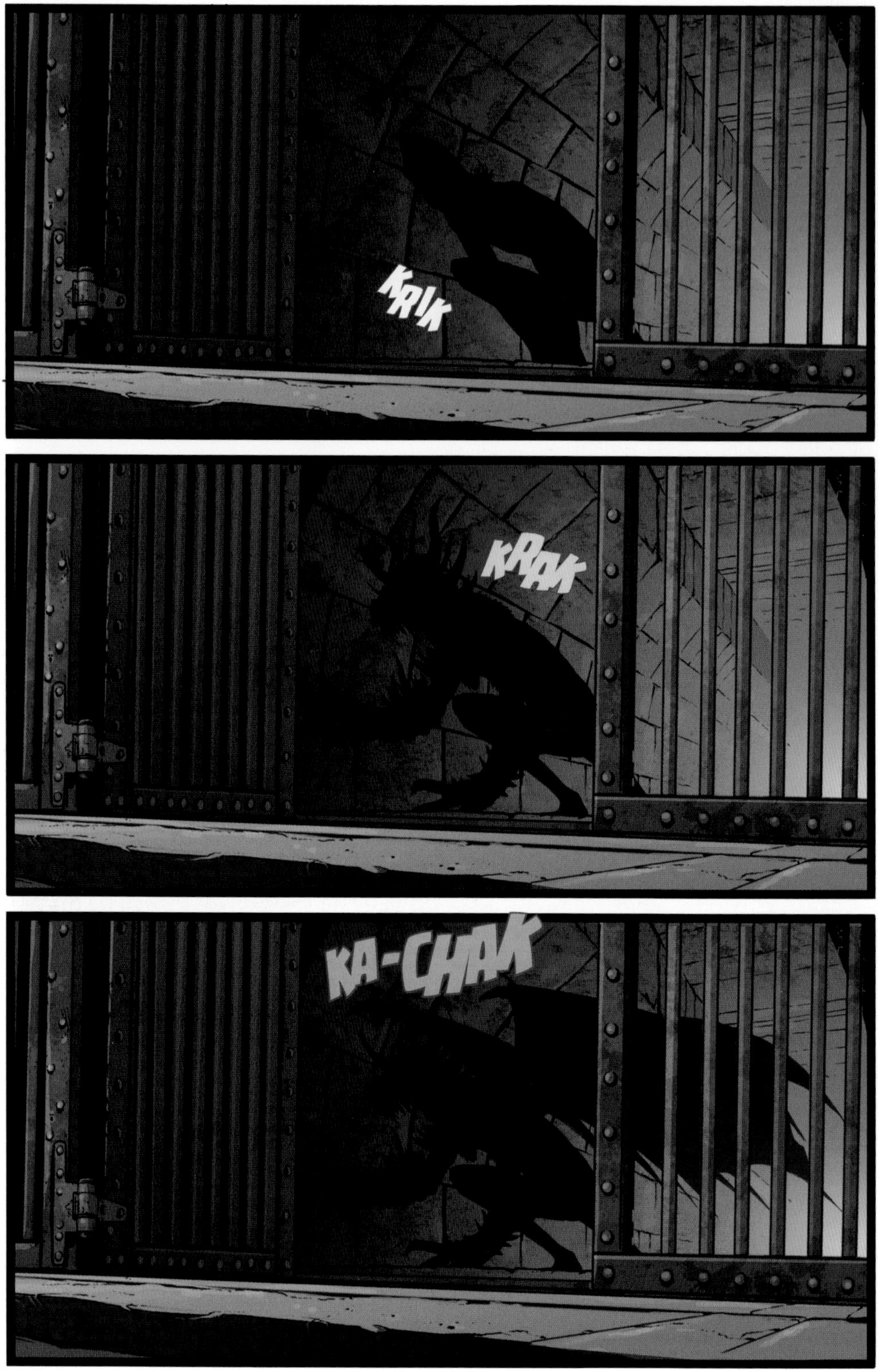
KRIK
KRAK
KA-CHAK

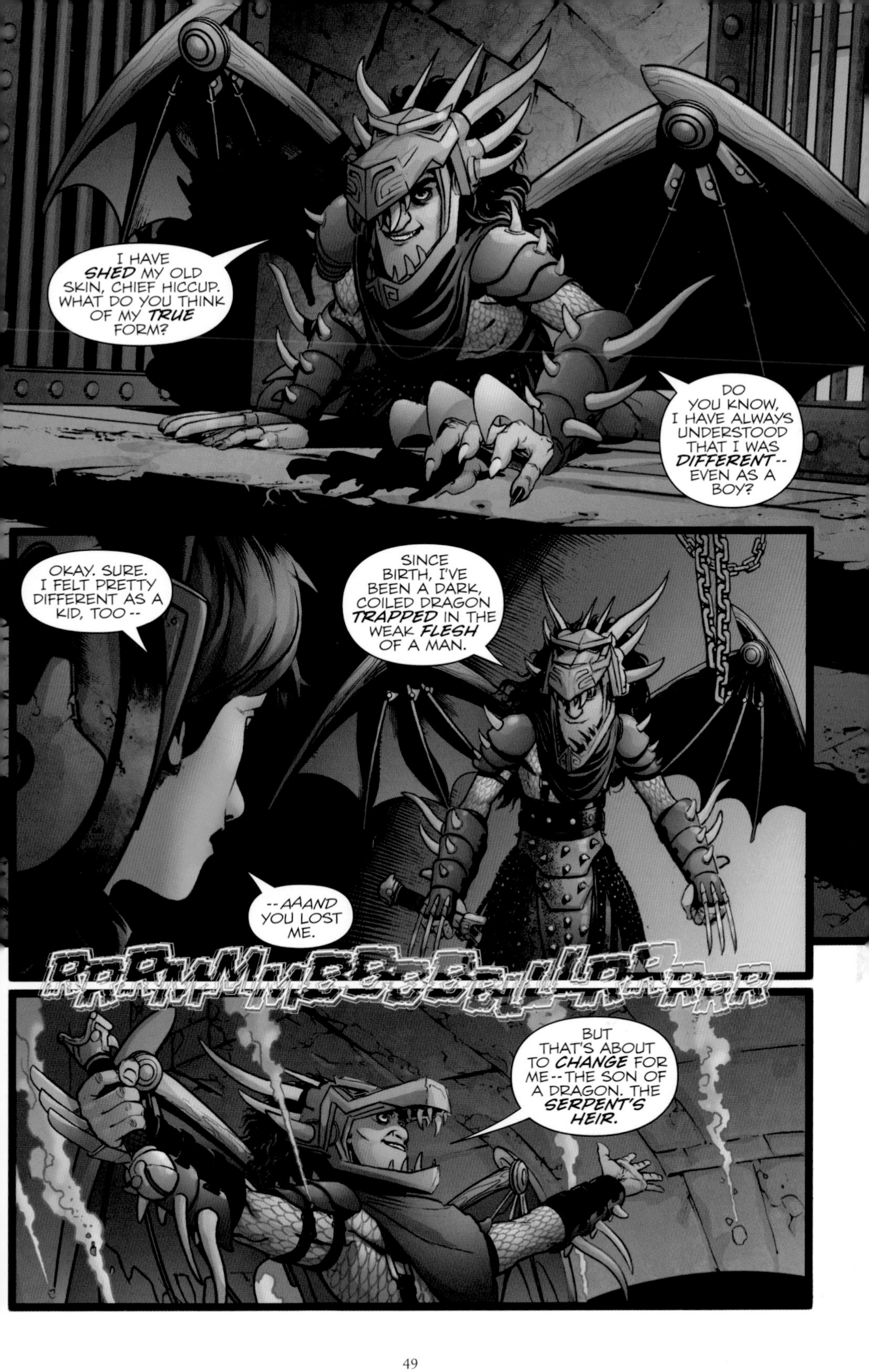
I HAVE SHED MY OLD SKIN, CHIEF HICCUP. WHAT DO YOU THINK OF MY TRUE FORM?
DO YOU KNOW, I HAVE ALWAYS UNDERSTOOD THAT I WAS DIFFERENT-- EVEN AS A BOY?
OKAY. SURE. I FELT PRETTY DIFFERENT AS A KID, TOO--
SINCE BIRTH, I'VE BEEN A DARK, COILED DRAGON TRAPPED IN THE WEAK FLESH OF A MAN.
--AAAND YOU LOST ME.
BUT THAT'S ABOUT TO CHANGE FOR ME--THE SON OF A DRAGON. THE SERPENT'S HEIR.

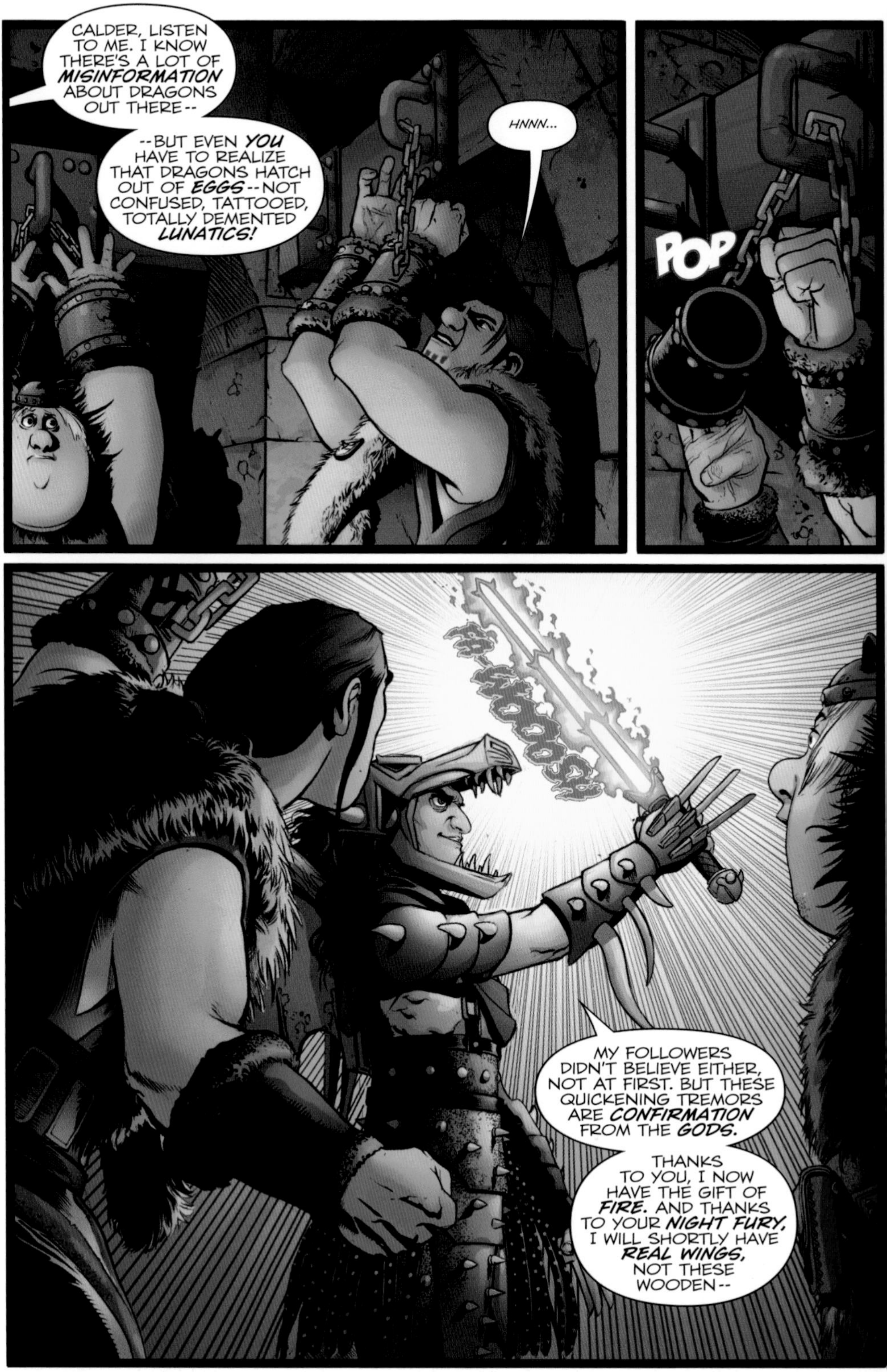
CALDER, LISTEN TO ME. I KNOW THERE'S A LOT OF MISINFORMATION ABOUT DRAGONS OUT THERE--
--BUT EVEN YOU HAVE TO REALIZE THAT DRAGONS HATCH OUT OF EGGS--NOT CONFUSED, TATTOOED, TOTALLY DEMENTED LUNATICS!
HNNN...
POP
MY FOLLOWERS DIDN'T BELIEVE EITHER, NOT AT FIRST. BUT THESE QUICKENING TREMORS ARE CONFIRMATION FROM THE GODS.
THANKS TO YOU, I NOW HAVE THE GIFT OF FIRE. AND THANKS TO YOUR NIGHT FURY, I WILL SHORTLY HAVE REAL WINGS, NOT THESE WOODEN--

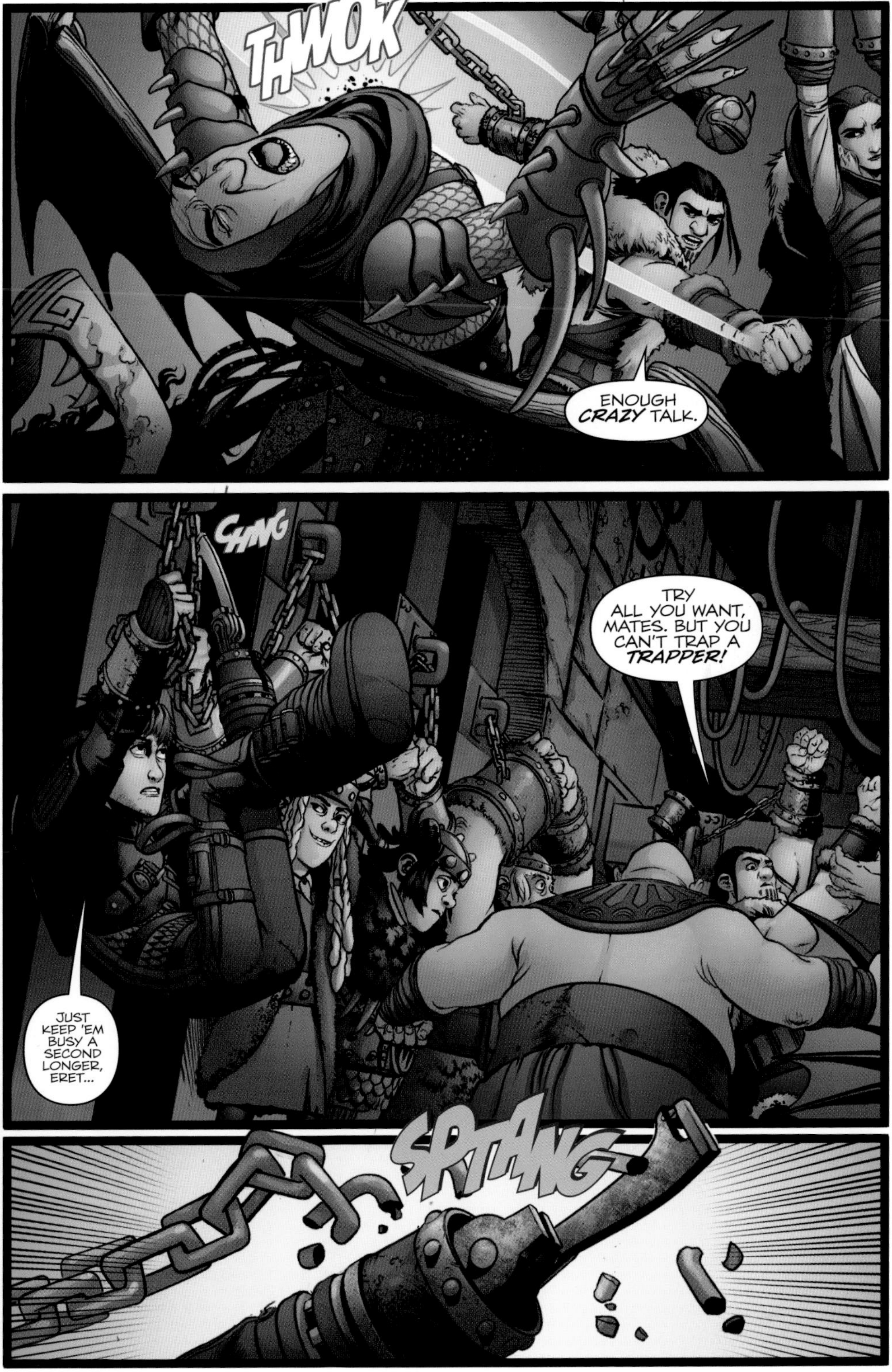
THWOK
ENOUGH CRAZY TALK.
CHING
TRY ALL YOU WANT, MATES. BUT YOU CAN'T TRAP A TRAPPER!
JUST KEEP 'EM BUSY A SECOND LONGER, ERET...
SPTANG

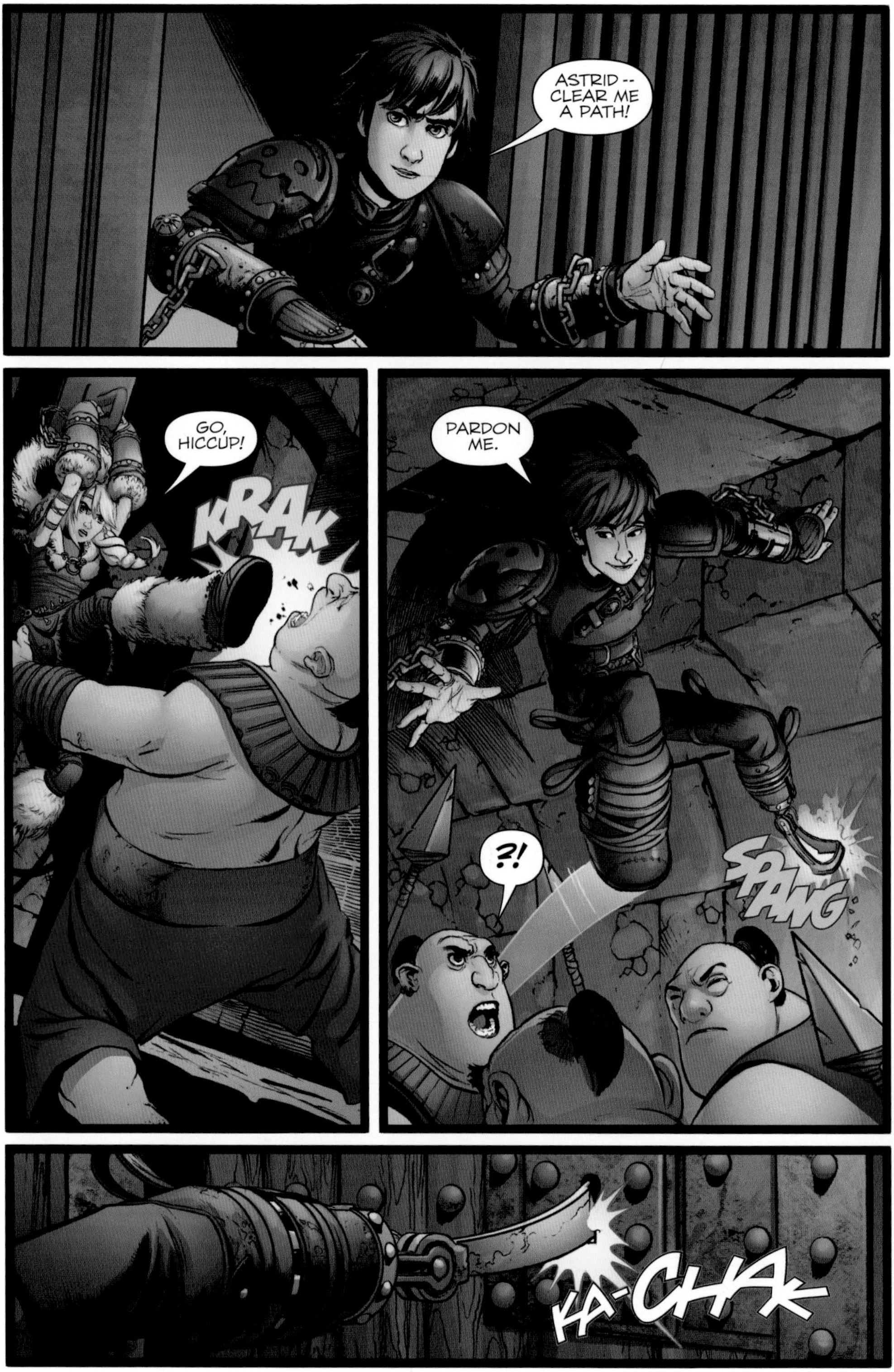
ASTRID -- CLEAR ME A PATH!
GO, HICCUP!
KRAK
PARDON ME.
?!
SPANG
KA-CHAK

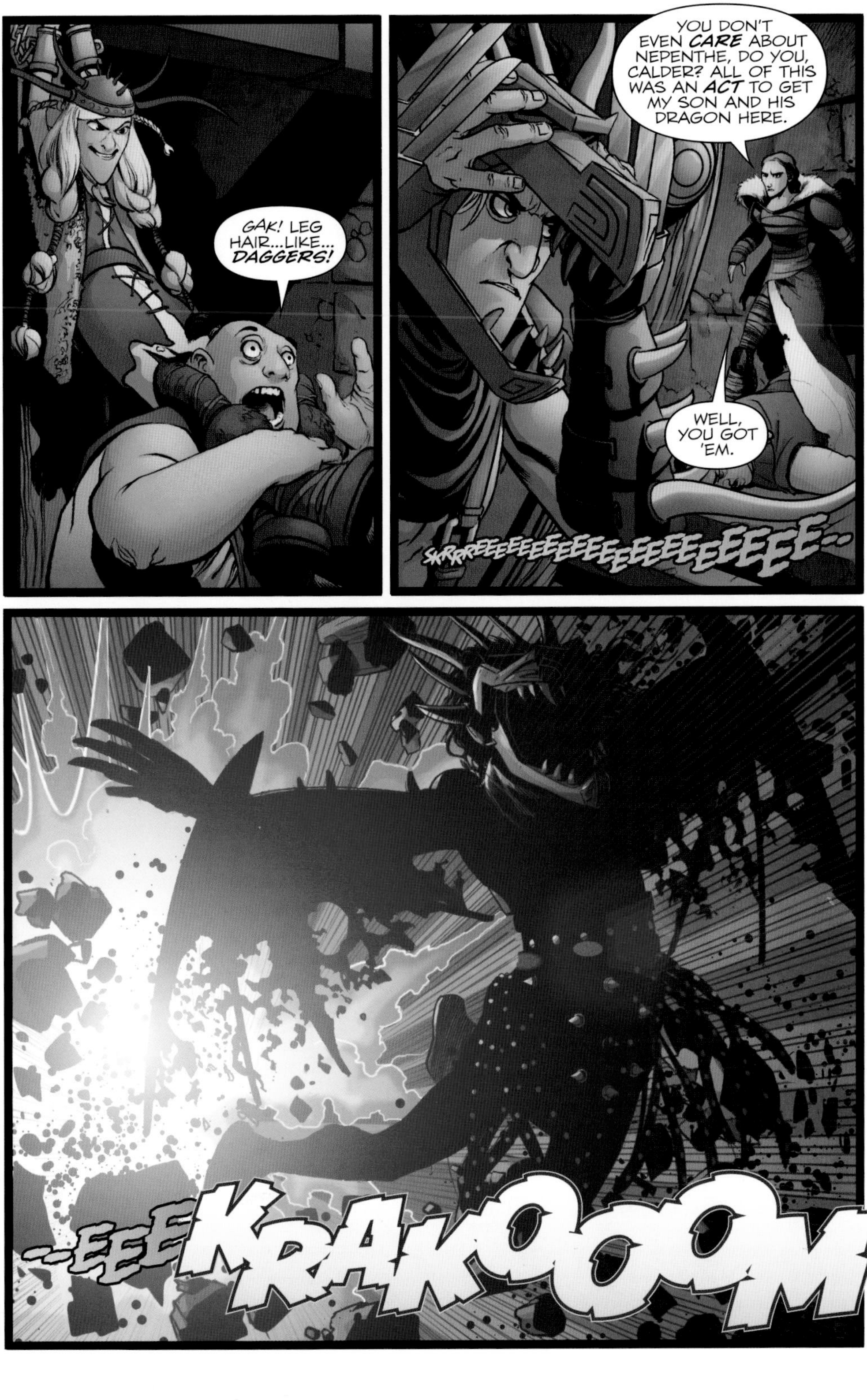
GAK! LEG HAIR...LIKE... DAGGERS!
YOU DON'T EVEN CARE ABOUT NEPENTHE, DO YOU, CALDER? ALL OF THIS WAS AN ACT TO GET MY SON AND HIS DRAGON HERE.
WELL, YOU GOT 'EM.
SKRRREEEEEEEEEEEEEEEEEEEEEEEE--
--EEEKRAKOOOM

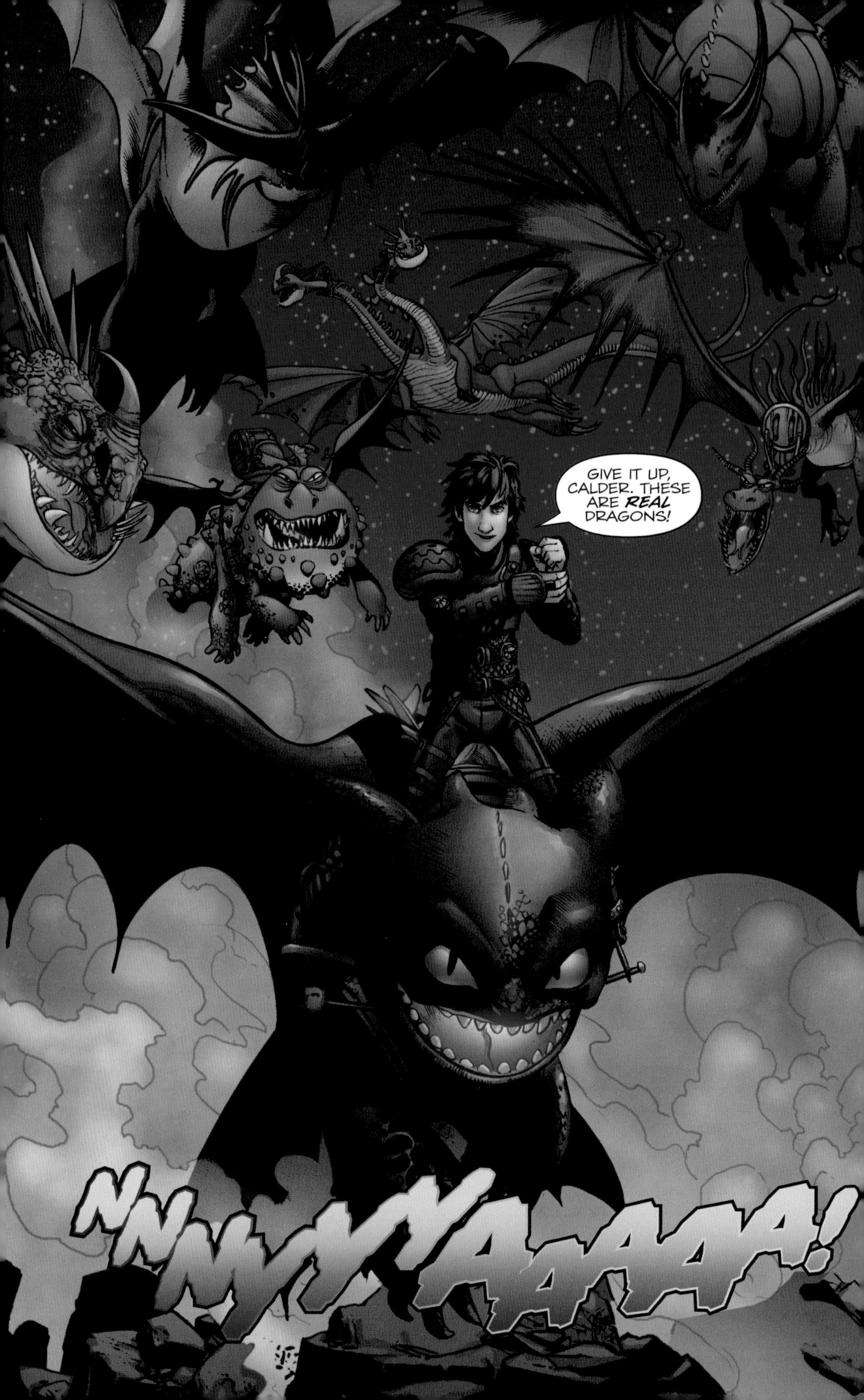
GIVE IT UP, CALDER. THESE ARE *REAL* DRAGONS!
NNNYYAAAAA!

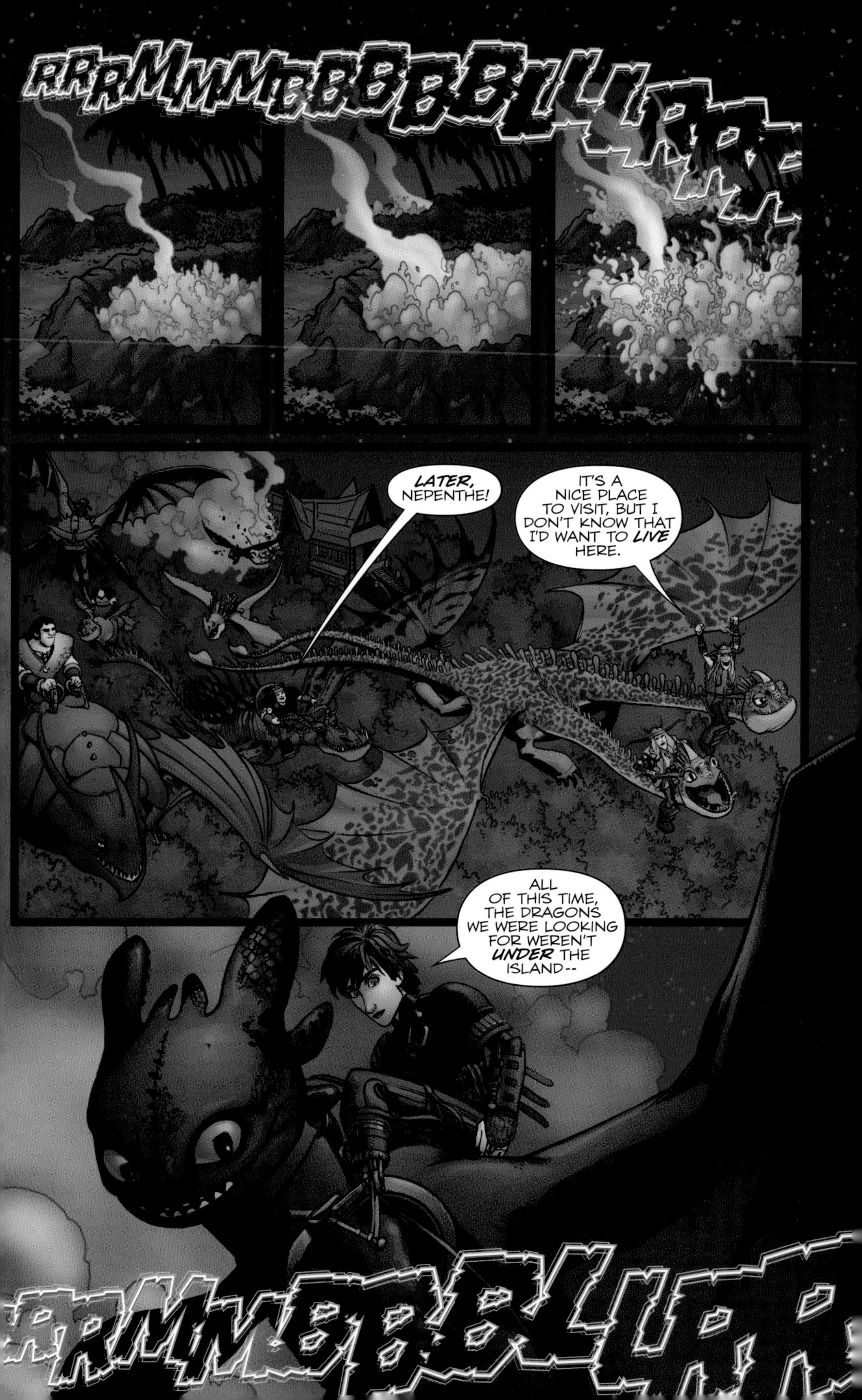
RRRMMMBBBBLLRRR
LATER, NEPENTHE!
IT'S A NICE PLACE TO VISIT, BUT I DON'T KNOW THAT I'D WANT TO LIVE HERE.
ALL OF THIS TIME, THE DRAGONS WE WERE LOOKING FOR WEREN'T UNDER THE ISLAND--
RMMBBLLRR

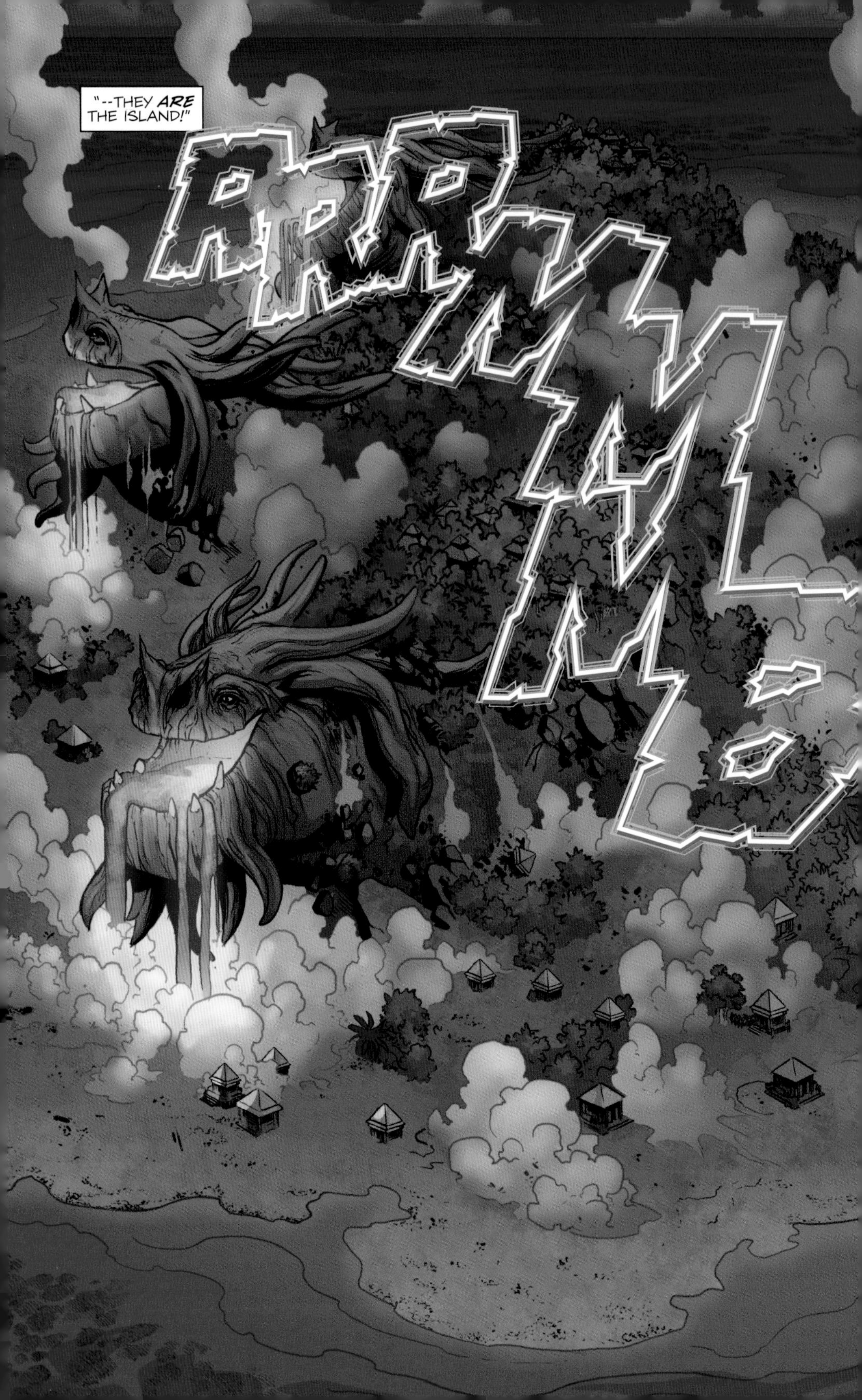
"--THEY *ARE* THE ISLAND!"

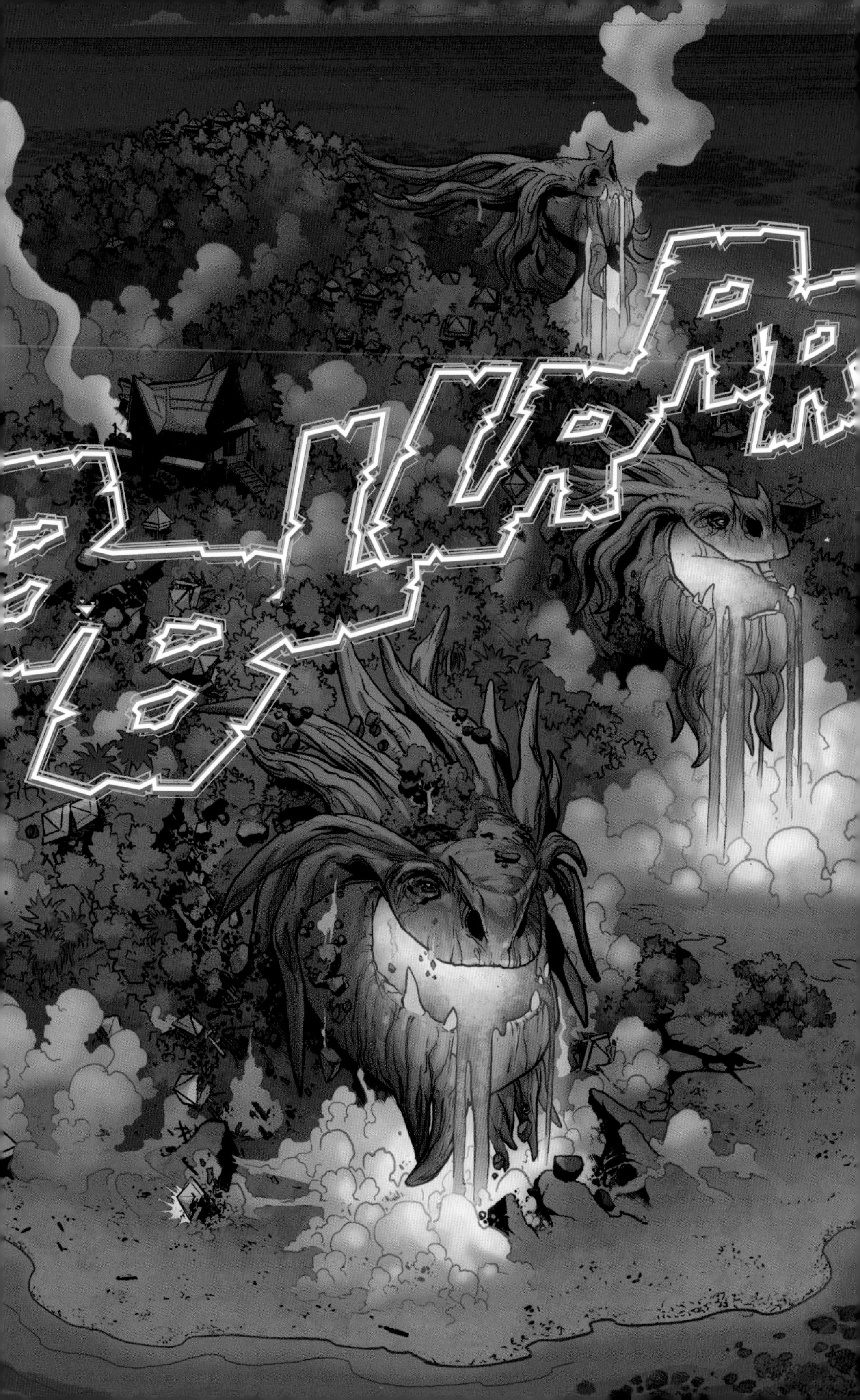

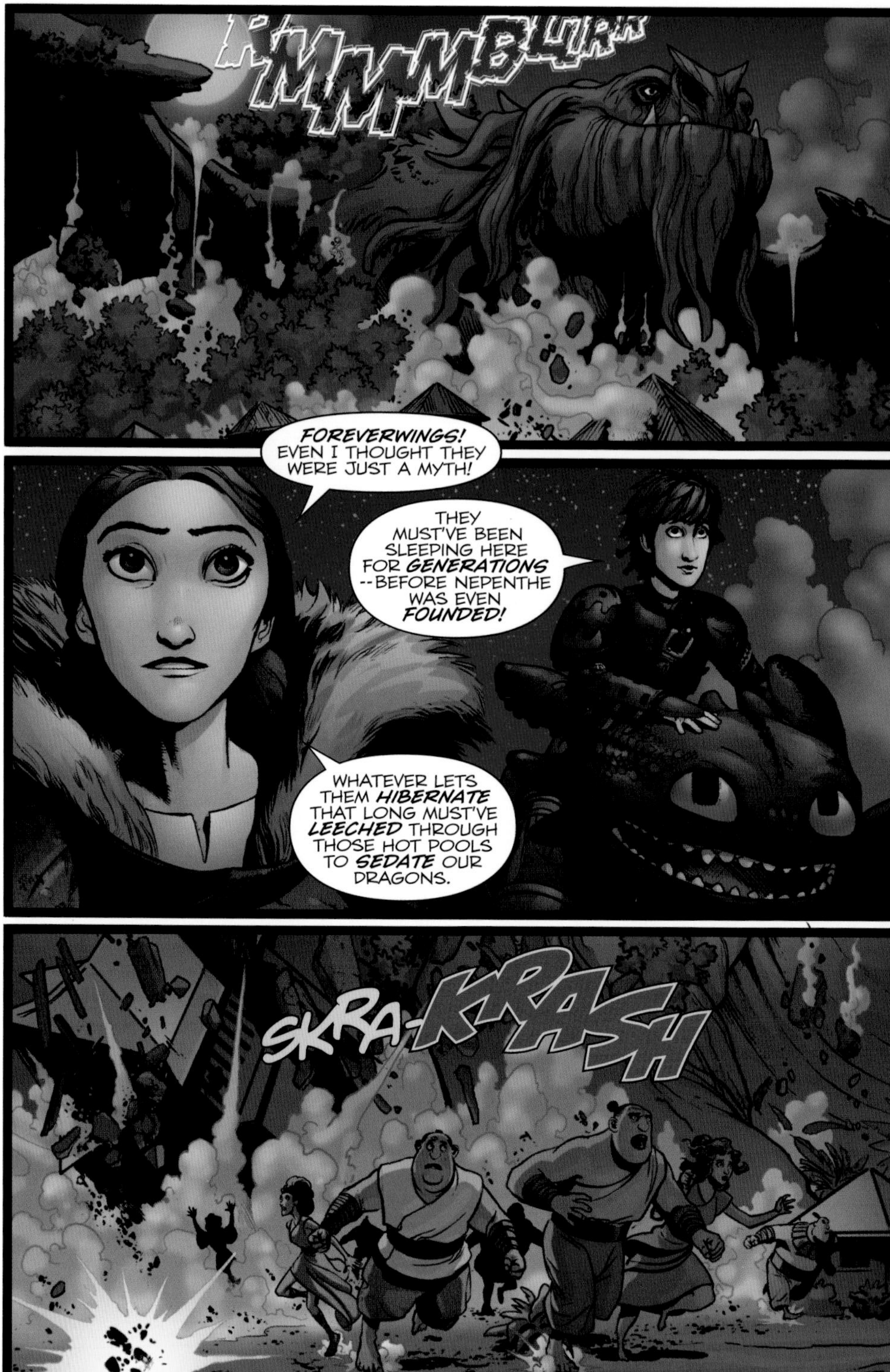

RMMMBLRR
FOREVERWINGS! EVEN I THOUGHT THEY WERE JUST A MYTH!
THEY MUST'VE BEEN SLEEPING HERE FOR GENERATIONS --BEFORE NEPENTHE WAS EVEN FOUNDED!
WHATEVER LETS THEM HIBERNATE THAT LONG MUST'VE LEECHED THROUGH THOSE HOT POOLS TO SEDATE OUR DRAGONS.
SKRA-KRASH

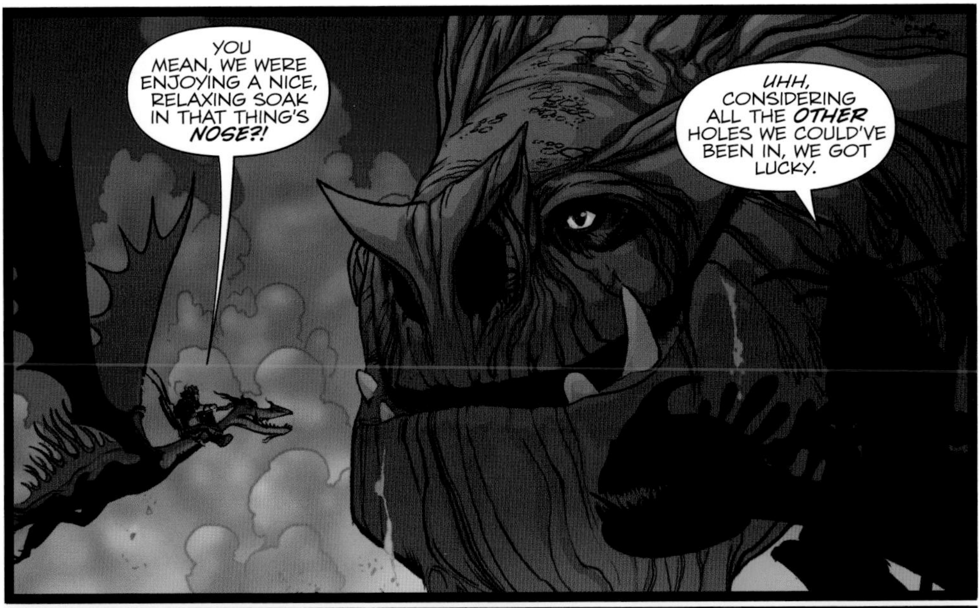
YOU MEAN, WE WERE ENJOYING A NICE, RELAXING SOAK IN THAT THING'S *NOSE?!*
UHH, CONSIDERING ALL THE *OTHER* HOLES WE COULD'VE BEEN IN, WE GOT LUCKY.

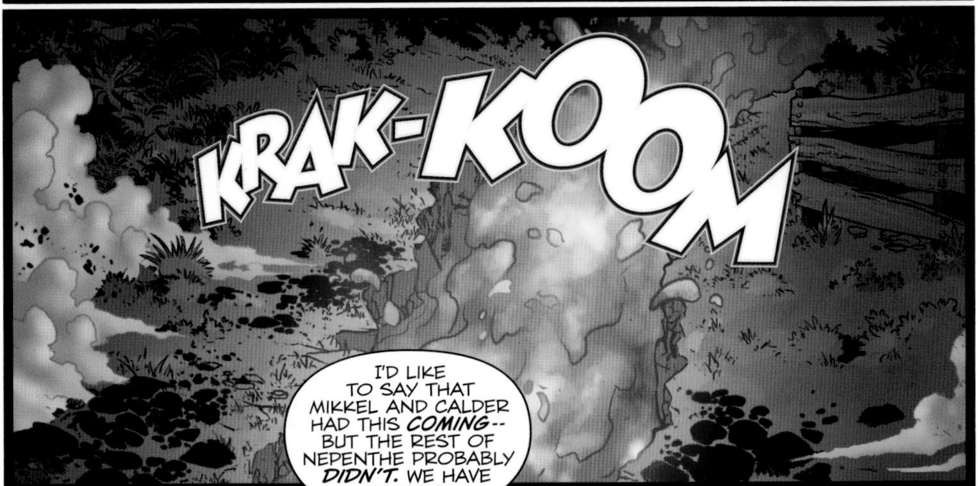
KRAK-KOOOM
I'D LIKE TO SAY THAT MIKKEL AND CALDER HAD THIS *COMING*-- BUT THE REST OF NEPENTHE PROBABLY *DIDN'T.* WE HAVE TO HELP.

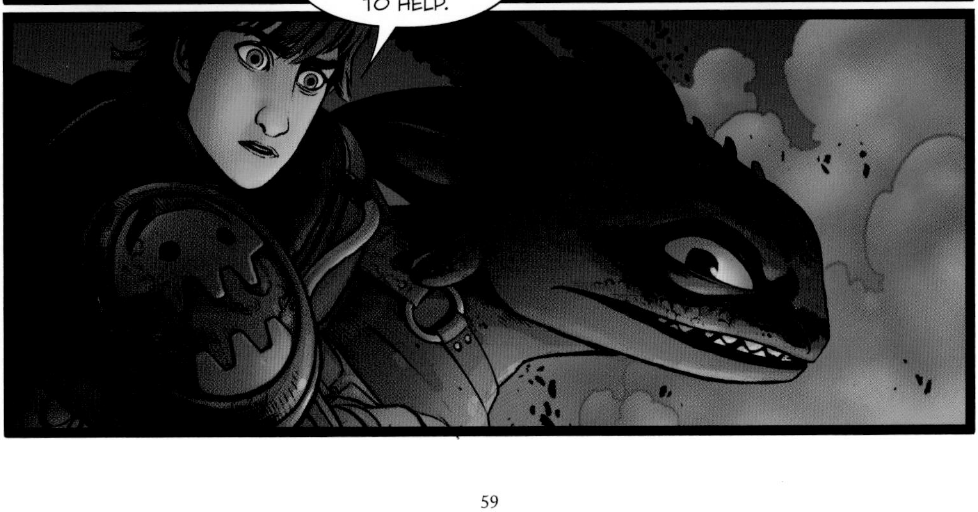

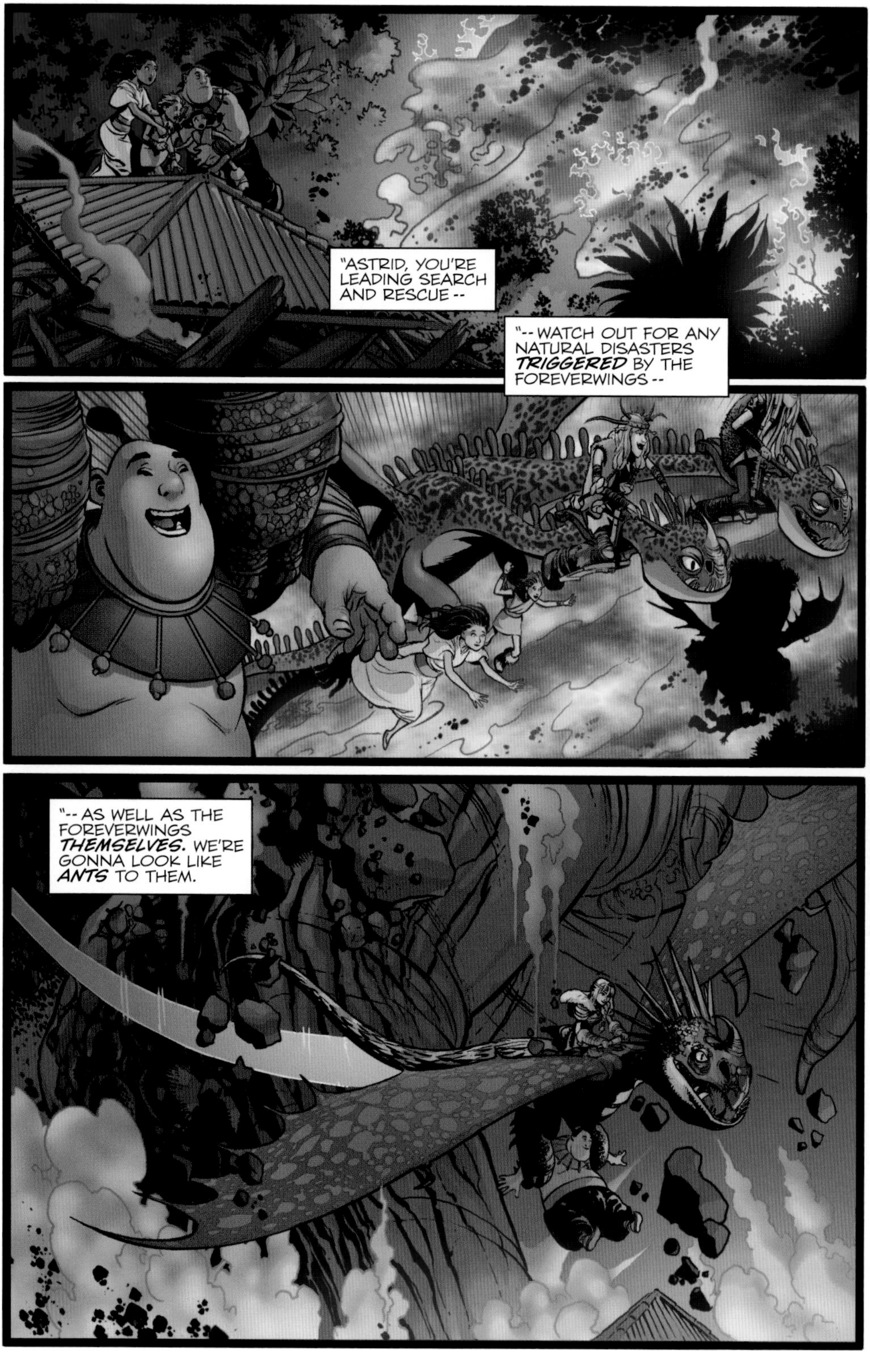
"ASTRID, YOU'RE LEADING SEARCH AND RESCUE --
"-- WATCH OUT FOR ANY NATURAL DISASTERS TRIGGERED BY THE FOREVERWINGS --
"-- AS WELL AS THE FOREVERWINGS THEMSELVES. WE'RE GONNA LOOK LIKE ANTS TO THEM.

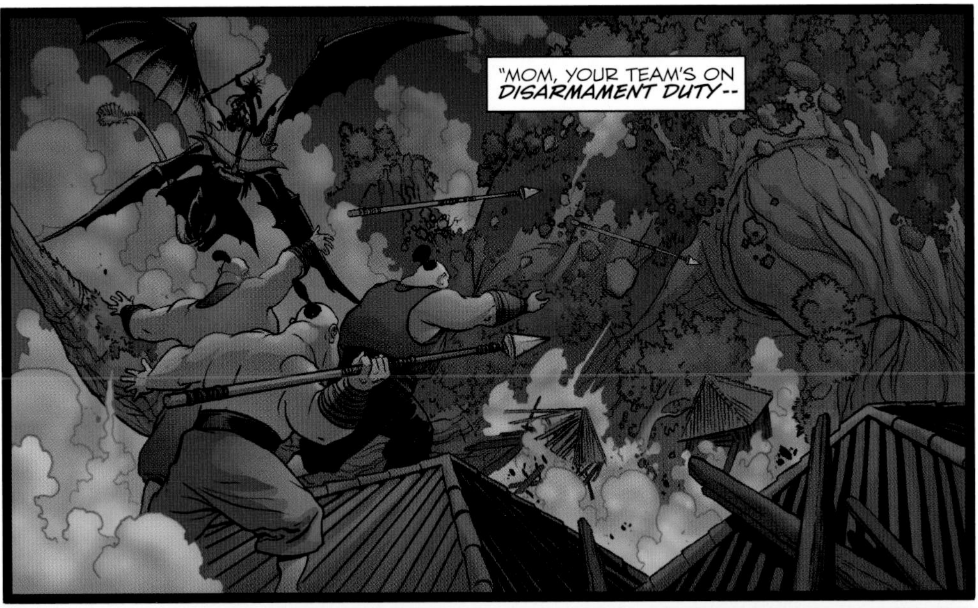
"MOM, YOUR TEAM'S ON DISARMAMENT DUTY--

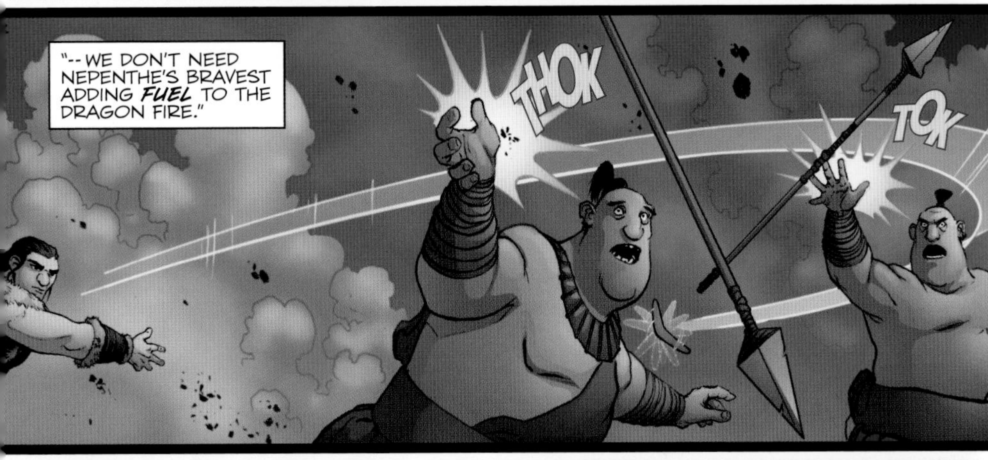
"--WE DON'T NEED NEPENTHE'S BRAVEST ADDING FUEL TO THE DRAGON FIRE."
THOK
TOK

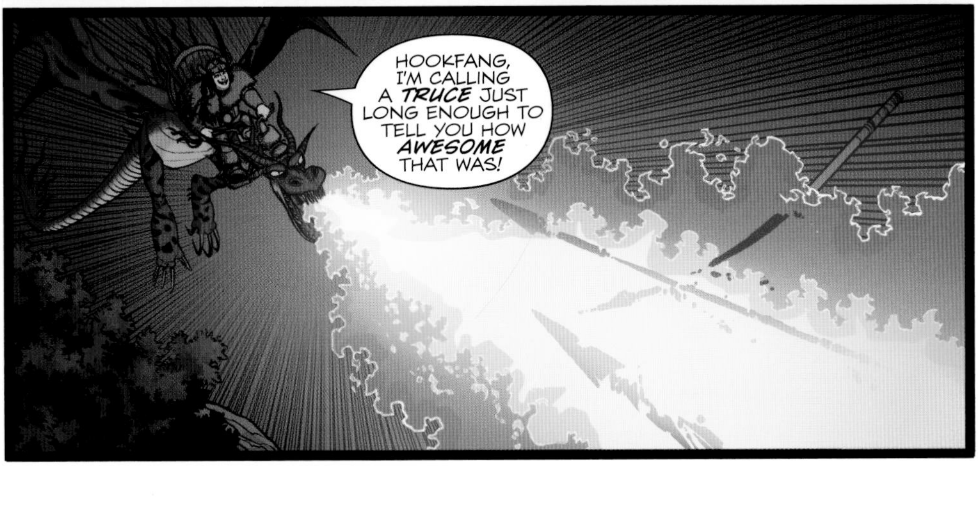
HOOKFANG, I'M CALLING A TRUCE JUST LONG ENOUGH TO TELL YOU HOW AWESOME THAT WAS!

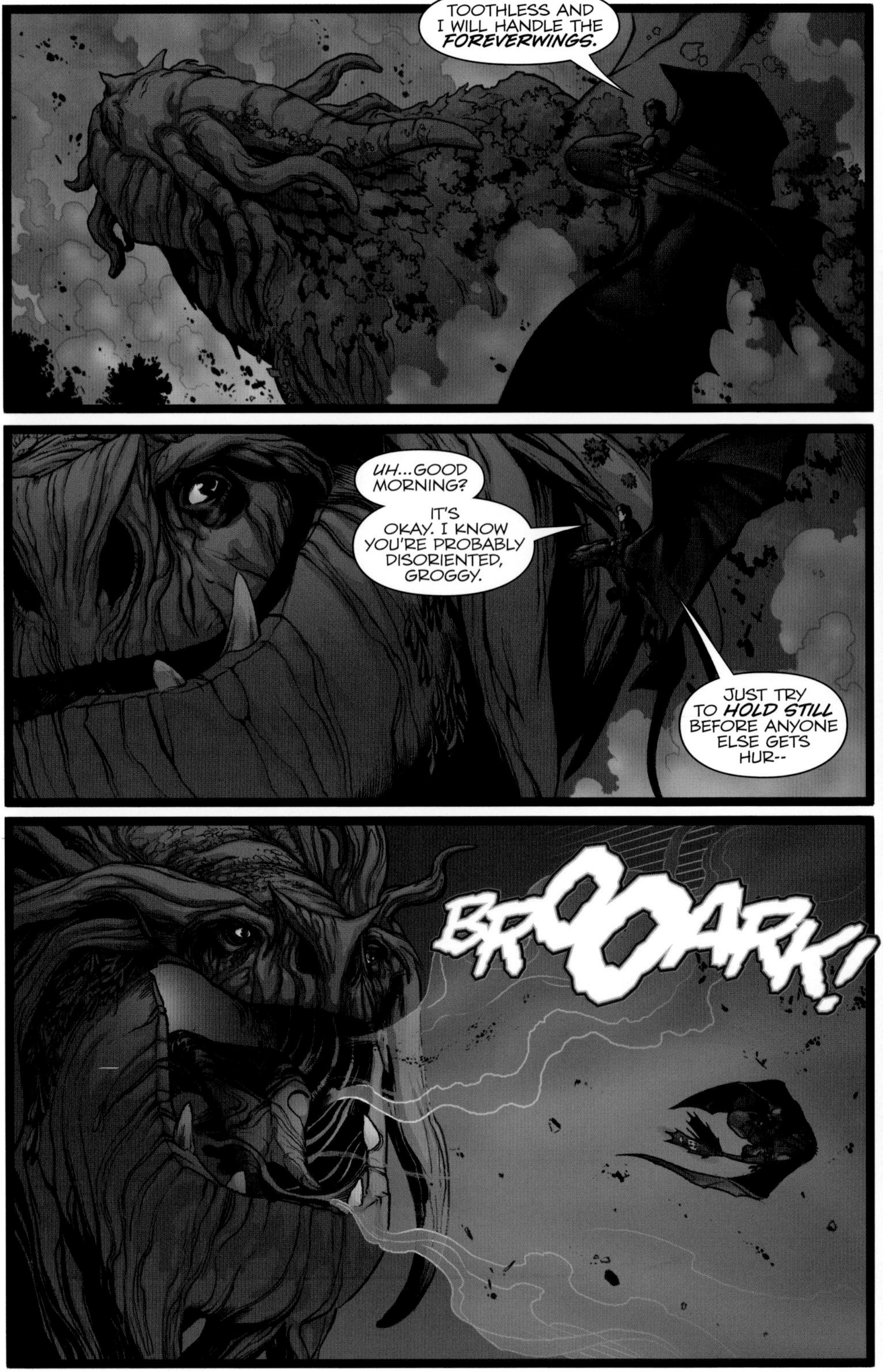
TOOTHLESS AND I WILL HANDLE THE FOREVERWINGS.
UH...GOOD MORNING?
IT'S OKAY. I KNOW YOU'RE PROBABLY DISORIENTED, GROGGY.
JUST TRY TO HOLD STILL BEFORE ANYONE ELSE GETS HUR--
BROOARK!

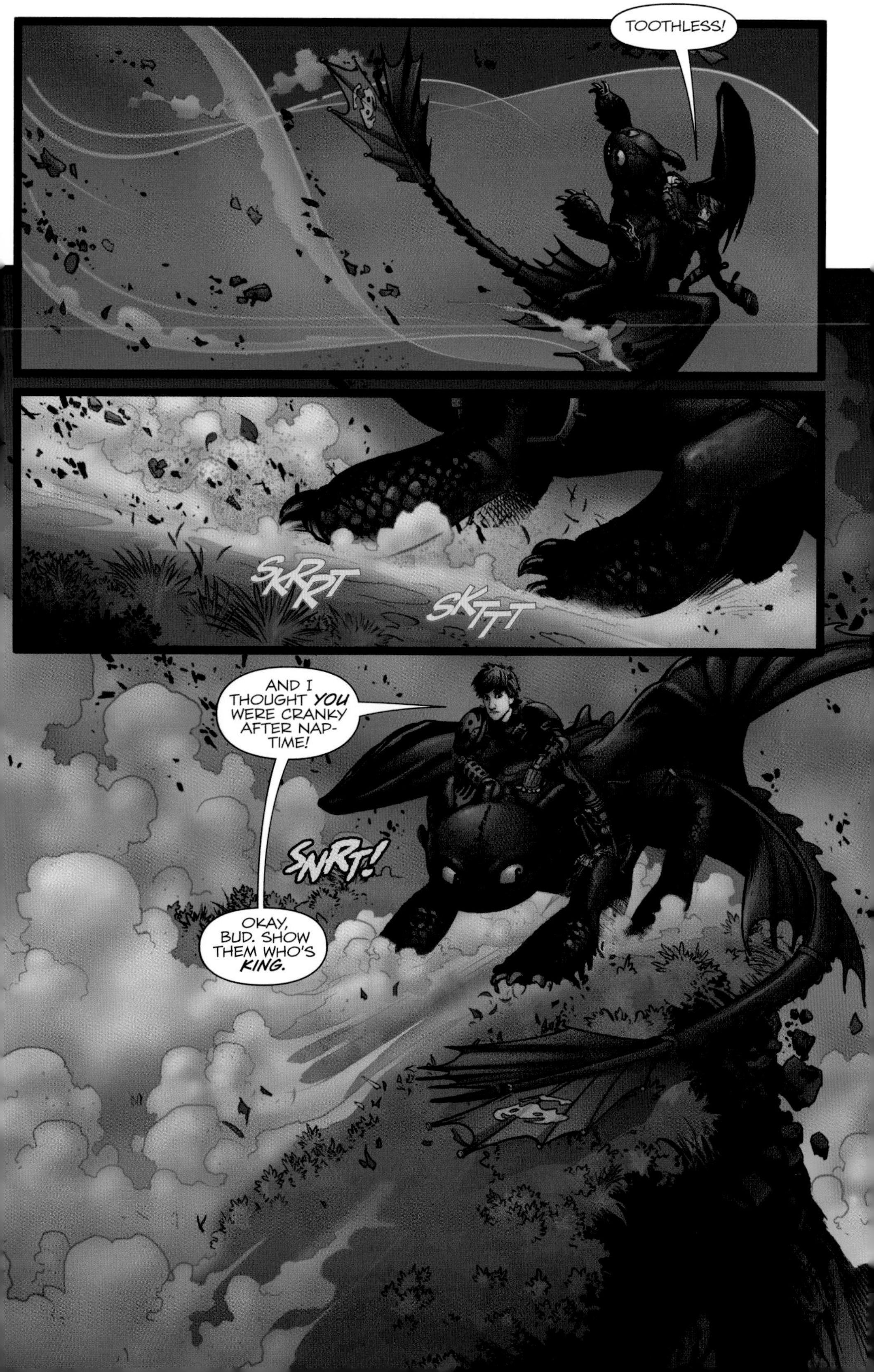
TOOTHLESS!
SKRRT
SKTTT
AND I THOUGHT YOU WERE CRANKY AFTER NAP-TIME!
SNRT!
OKAY, BUD. SHOW THEM WHO'S KING.

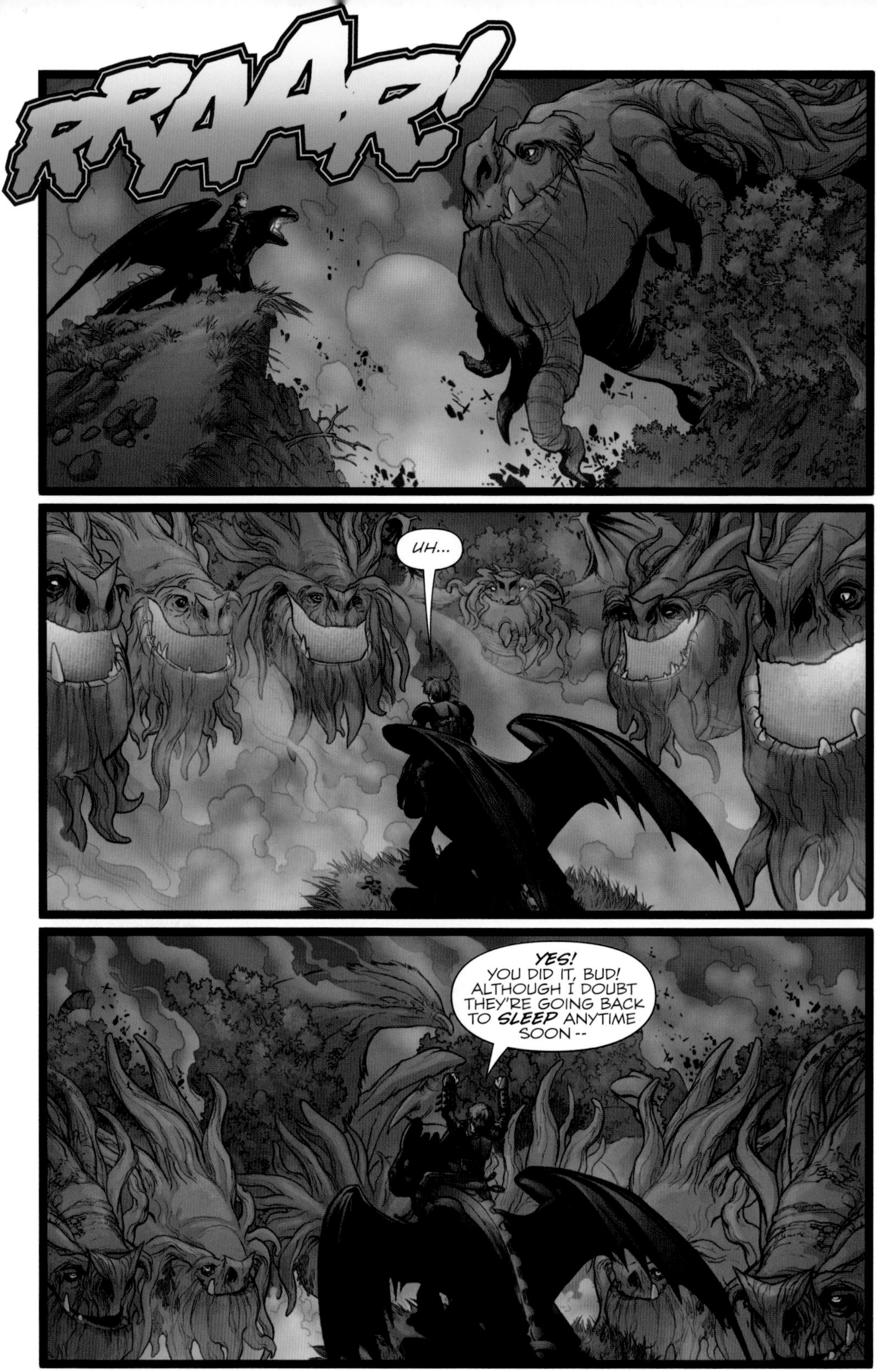
RRAAAR!
UH...
YES!
YOU DID IT, BUD!
ALTHOUGH I DOUBT
THEY'RE GOING BACK
TO SLEEP ANYTIME
SOON --

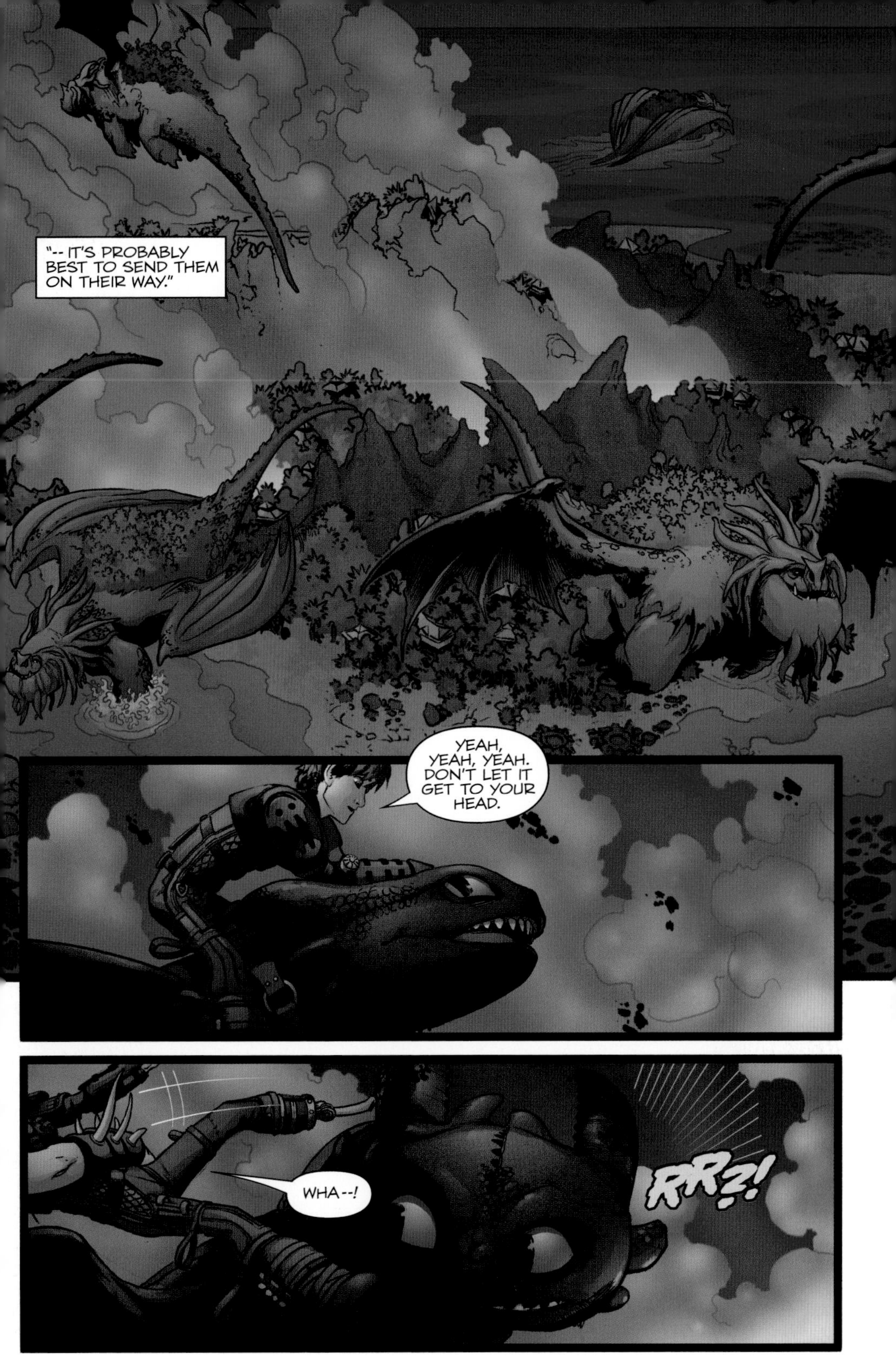
"-- IT'S PROBABLY BEST TO SEND THEM ON THEIR WAY."
YEAH, YEAH, YEAH. DON'T LET IT GET TO YOUR HEAD.
WHA--!
RRZ!

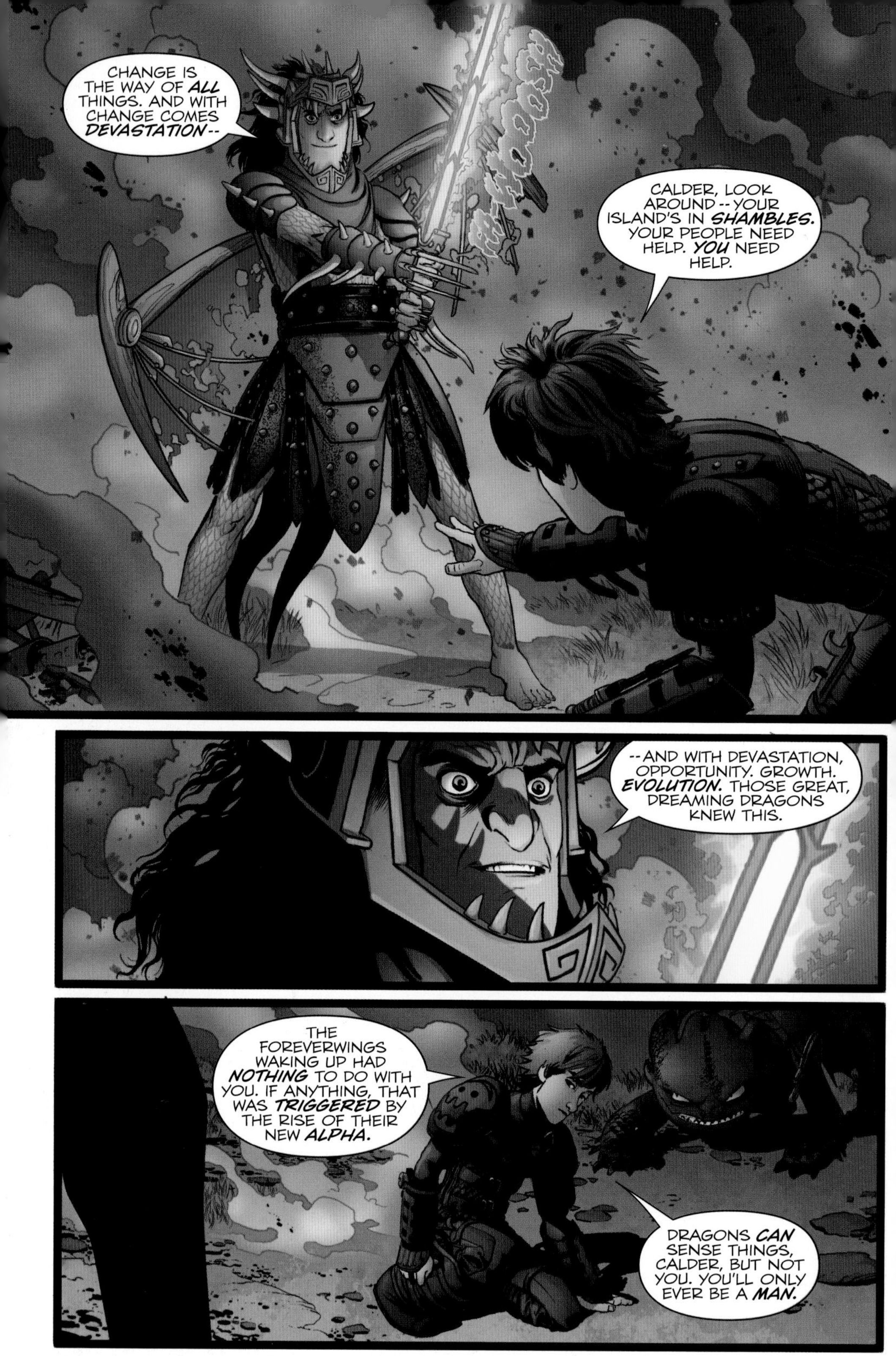
CHANGE IS THE WAY OF ALL THINGS. AND WITH CHANGE COMES DEVASTATION--
CALDER, LOOK AROUND--YOUR ISLAND'S IN SHAMBLES. YOUR PEOPLE NEED HELP. YOU NEED HELP.
--AND WITH DEVASTATION, OPPORTUNITY. GROWTH. EVOLUTION. THOSE GREAT, DREAMING DRAGONS KNEW THIS.
THE FOREVERWINGS WAKING UP HAD NOTHING TO DO WITH YOU. IF ANYTHING, THAT WAS TRIGGERED BY THE RISE OF THEIR NEW ALPHA.
DRAGONS CAN SENSE THINGS, CALDER, BUT NOT YOU. YOU'LL ONLY EVER BE A MAN.

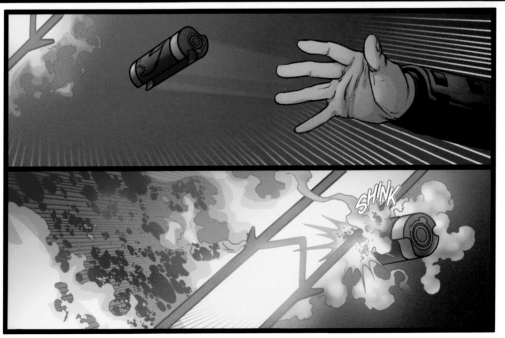

SHINK

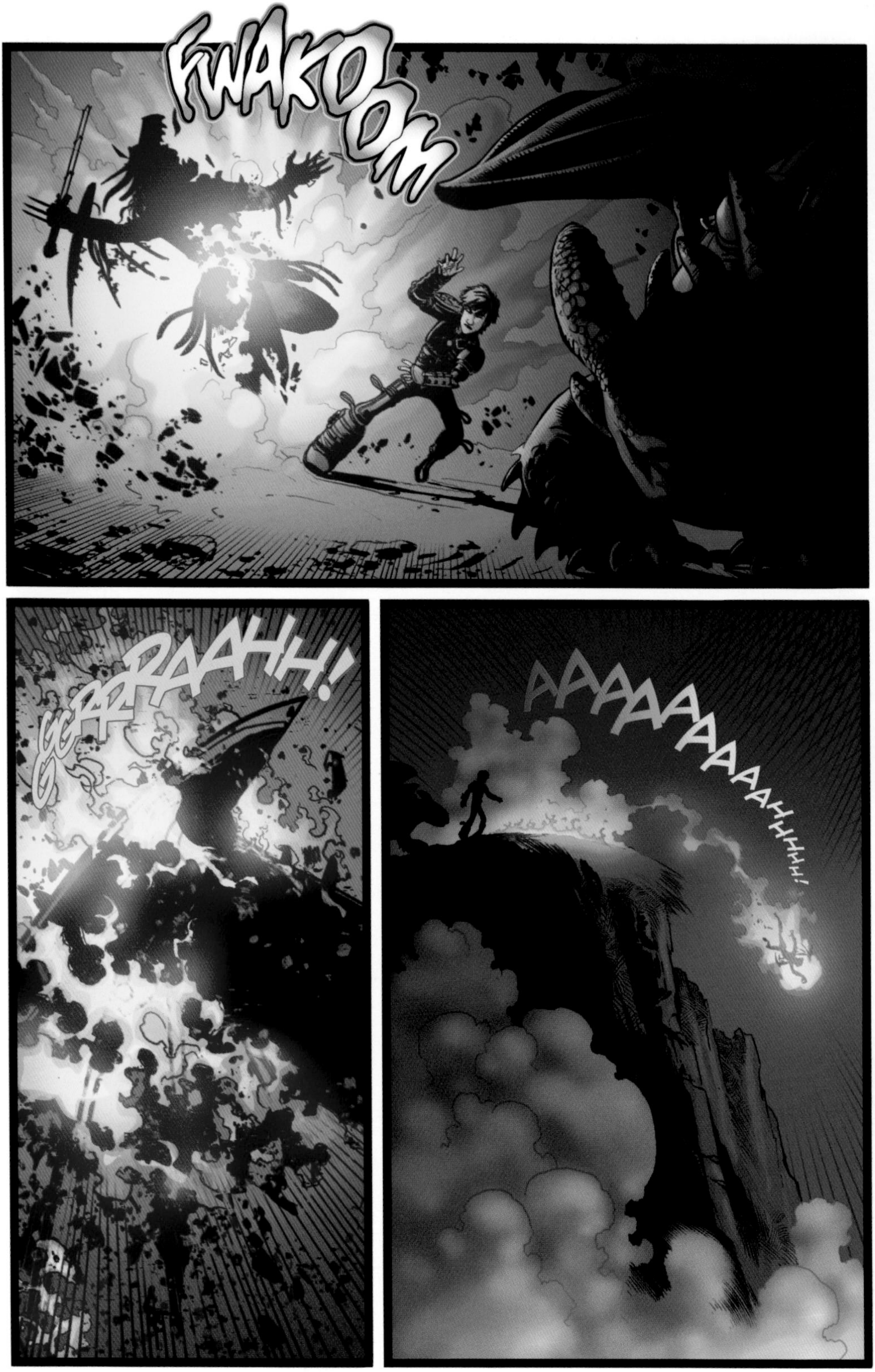
FWAKOOM
GGRRRAAHH!
AAAAAAAAAAAHHHH!

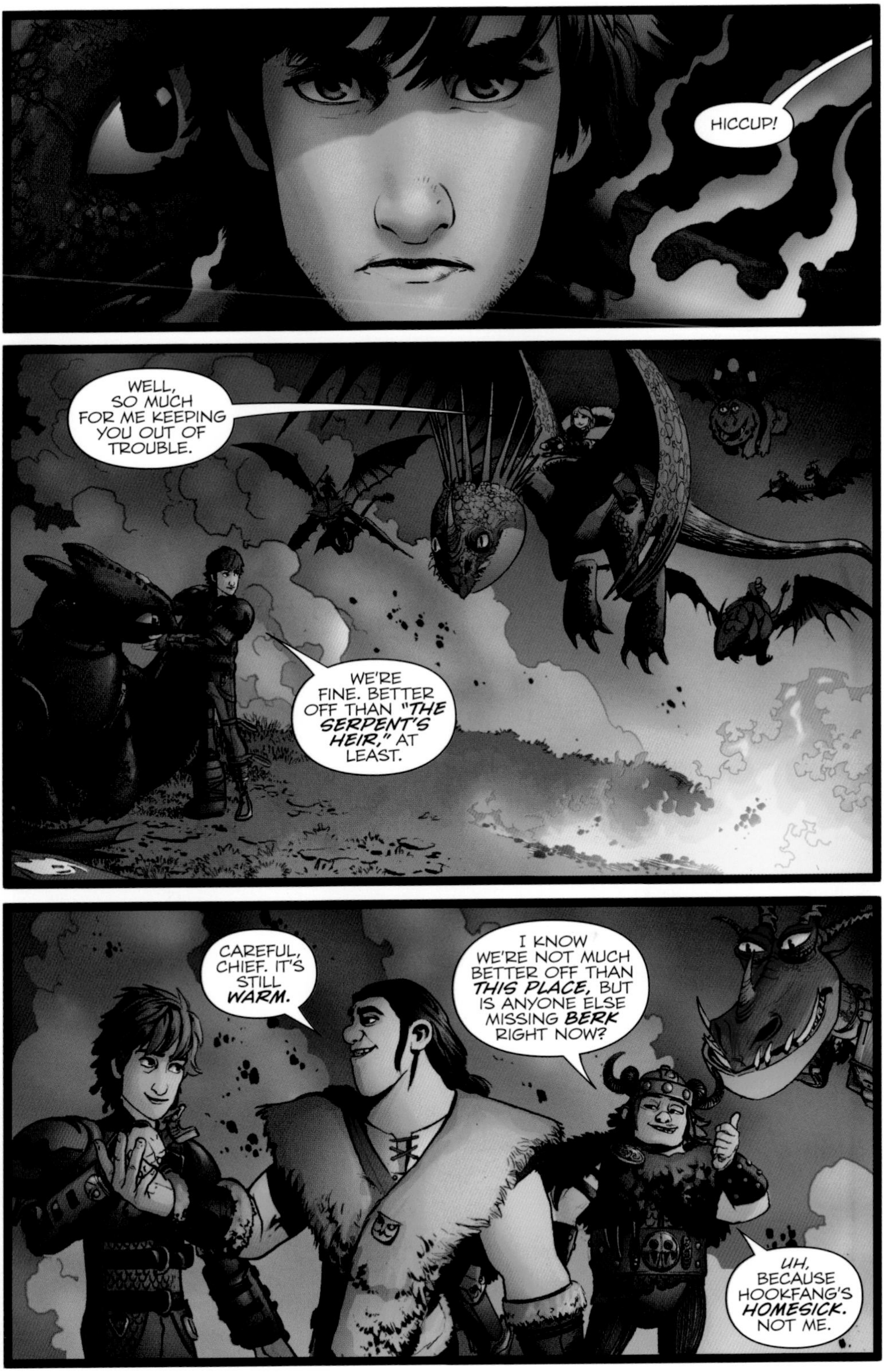
HICCUP!
WELL, SO MUCH FOR ME KEEPING YOU OUT OF TROUBLE.
WE'RE FINE. BETTER OFF THAN "THE SERPENT'S HEIR," AT LEAST.
CAREFUL, CHIEF. IT'S STILL WARM.
I KNOW WE'RE NOT MUCH BETTER OFF THAN THIS PLACE, BUT IS ANYONE ELSE MISSING BERK RIGHT NOW?
UH, BECAUSE HOOKFANG'S HOMESICK. NOT ME.

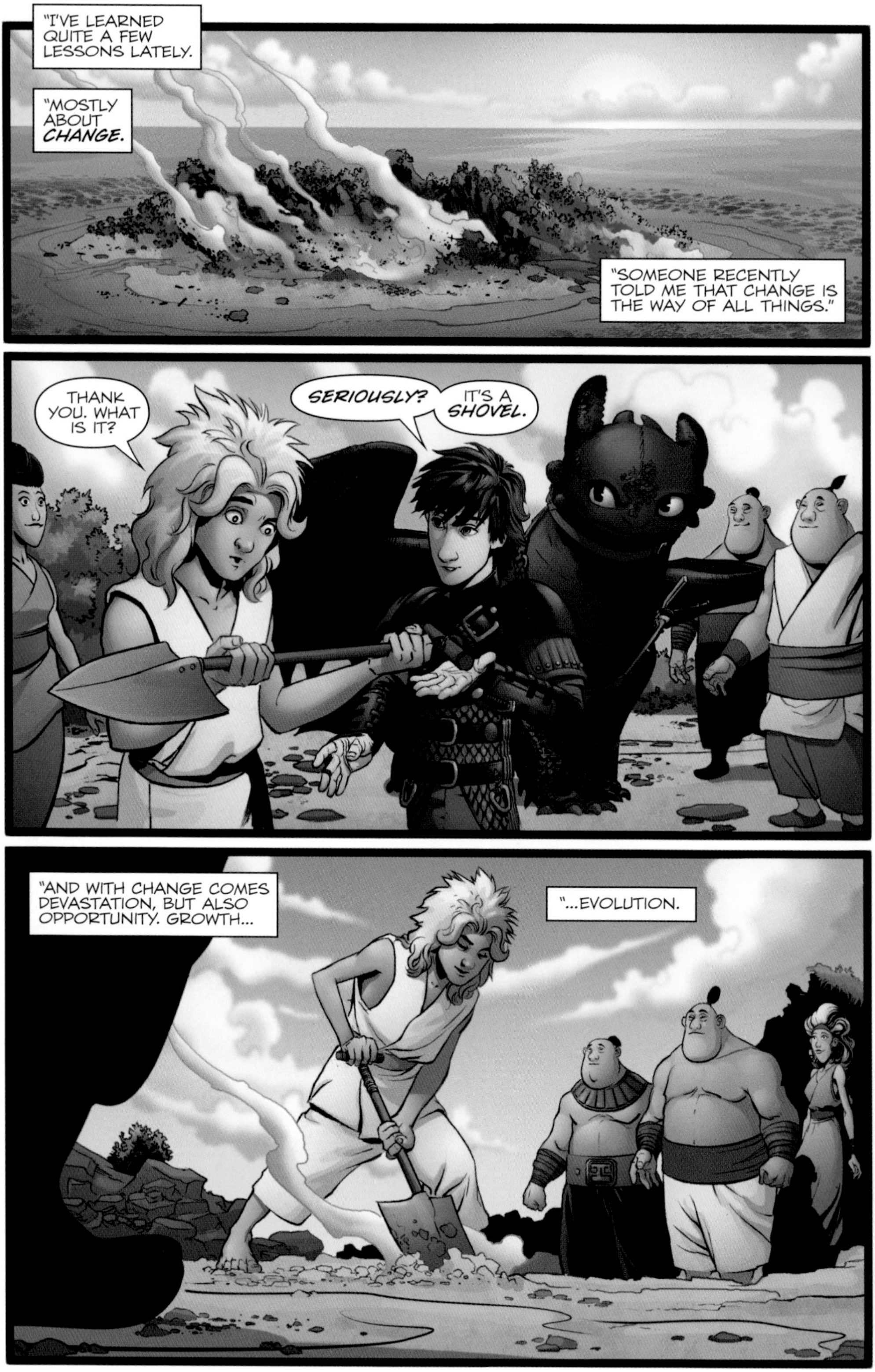
"I'VE LEARNED QUITE A FEW LESSONS LATELY.
"MOSTLY ABOUT ***CHANGE.***
"SOMEONE RECENTLY TOLD ME THAT CHANGE IS THE WAY OF ALL THINGS."
THANK YOU. WHAT IS IT?
SERIOUSLY?
IT'S A ***SHOVEL.***
"AND WITH CHANGE COMES DEVASTATION, BUT ALSO OPPORTUNITY. GROWTH...
"...EVOLUTION.

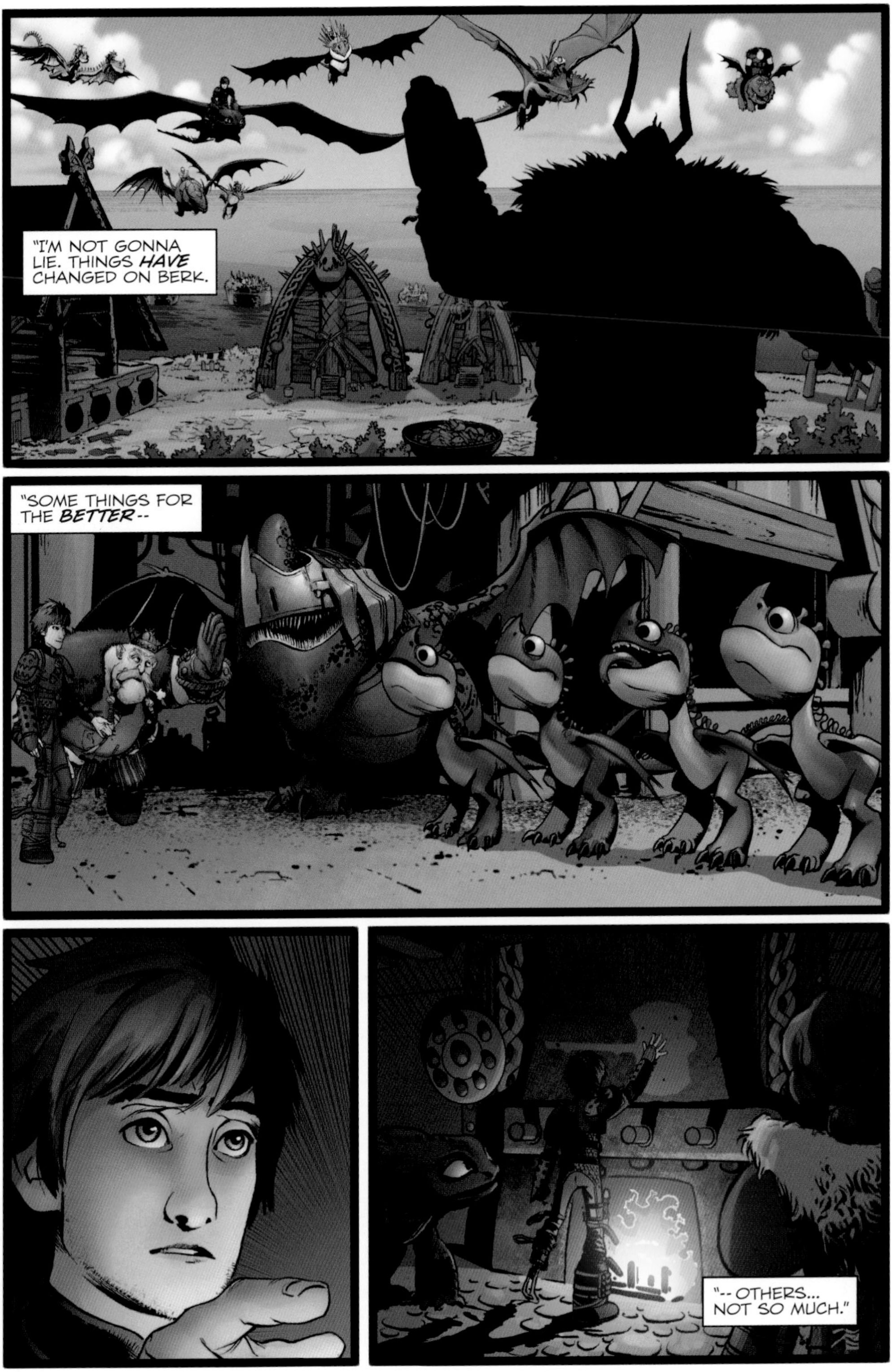
"I'M NOT GONNA LIE. THINGS *HAVE* CHANGED ON BERK.
"SOME THINGS FOR THE *BETTER*--
"-- OTHERS... NOT SO MUCH."

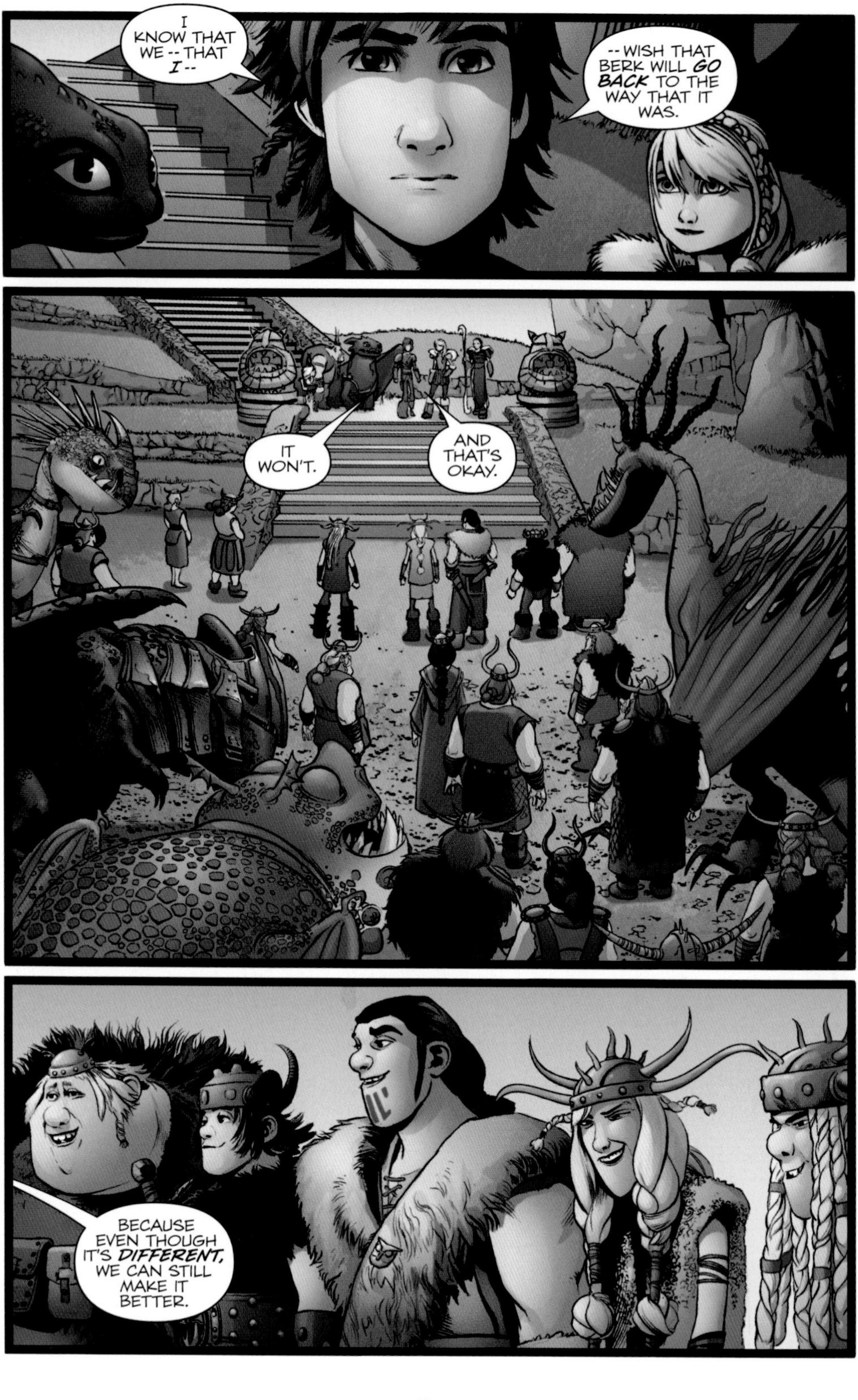
I KNOW THAT WE -- THAT I --
-- WISH THAT BERK WILL GO BACK TO THE WAY THAT IT WAS.
IT WON'T.
AND THAT'S OKAY.
BECAUSE EVEN THOUGH IT'S DIFFERENT, WE CAN STILL MAKE IT BETTER.

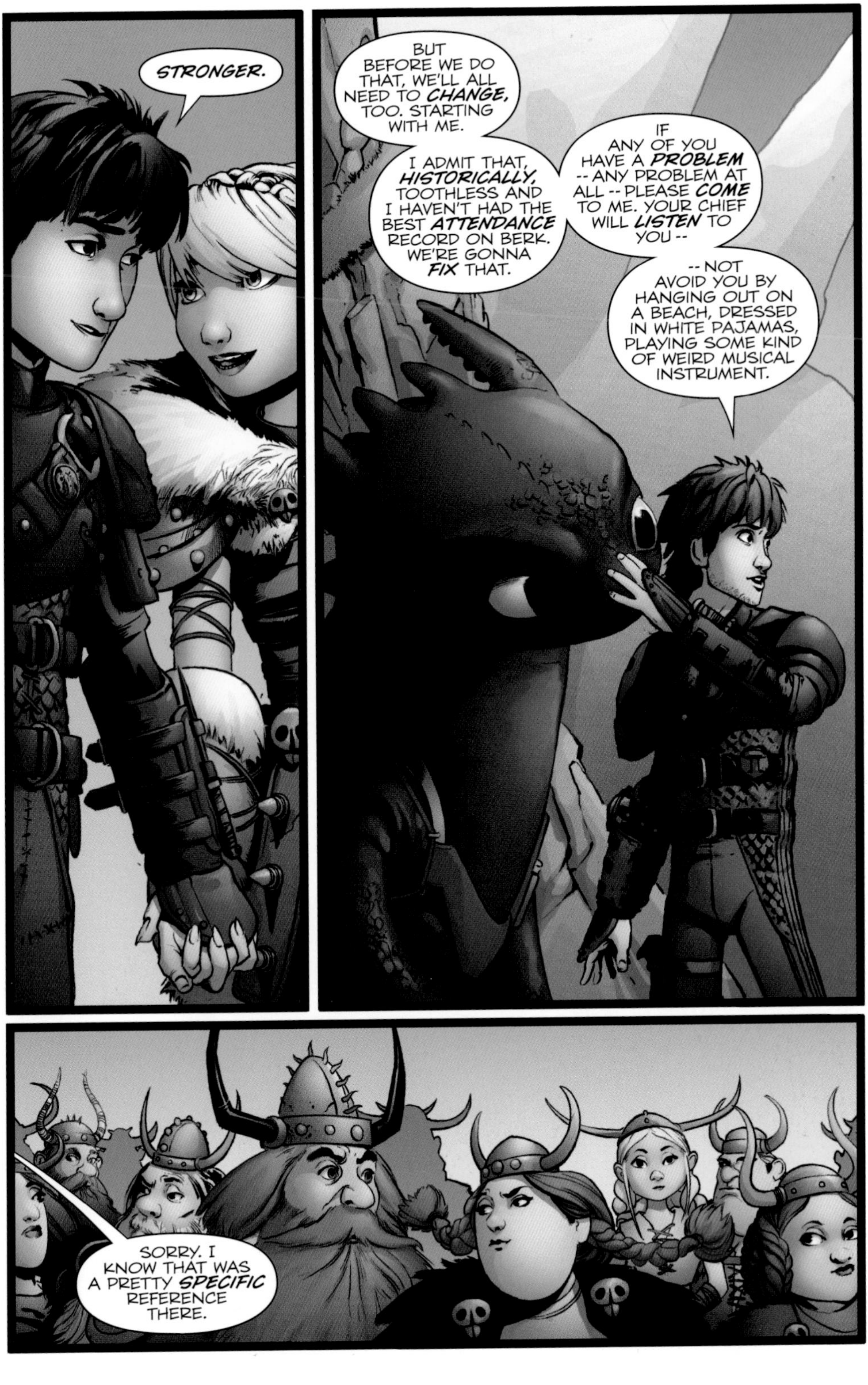
STRONGER.
BUT BEFORE WE DO THAT, WE'LL ALL NEED TO CHANGE, TOO. STARTING WITH ME.
I ADMIT THAT, HISTORICALLY, TOOTHLESS AND I HAVEN'T HAD THE BEST ATTENDANCE RECORD ON BERK. WE'RE GONNA FIX THAT.
IF ANY OF YOU HAVE A PROBLEM -- ANY PROBLEM AT ALL -- PLEASE COME TO ME. YOUR CHIEF WILL LISTEN TO YOU --
-- NOT AVOID YOU BY HANGING OUT ON A BEACH, DRESSED IN WHITE PAJAMAS, PLAYING SOME KIND OF WEIRD MUSICAL INSTRUMENT.
SORRY. I KNOW THAT WAS A PRETTY SPECIFIC REFERENCE THERE.

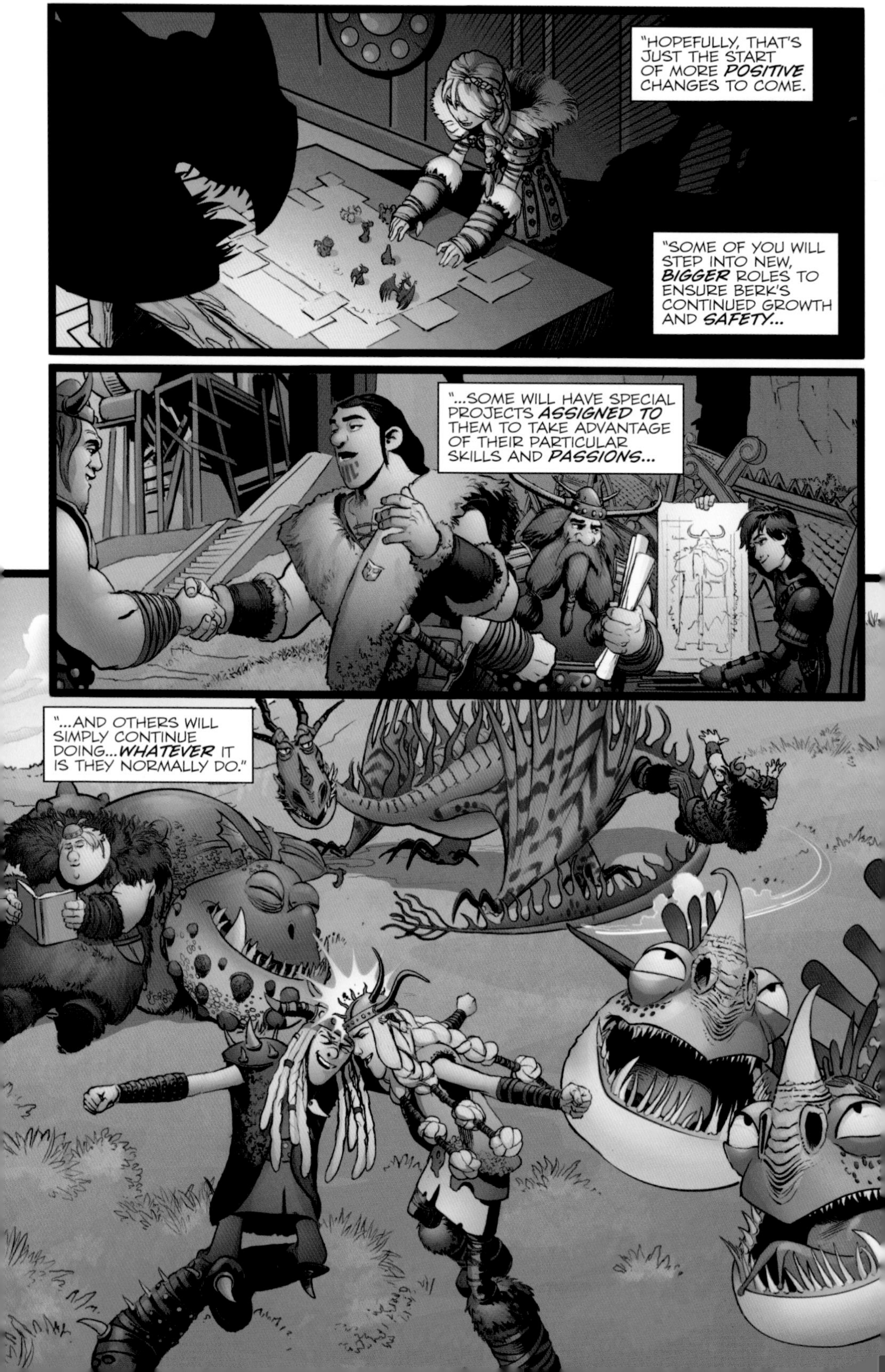
"HOPEFULLY, THAT'S JUST THE START OF MORE POSITIVE CHANGES TO COME.
"SOME OF YOU WILL STEP INTO NEW, BIGGER ROLES TO ENSURE BERK'S CONTINUED GROWTH AND SAFETY...
"...SOME WILL HAVE SPECIAL PROJECTS ASSIGNED TO THEM TO TAKE ADVANTAGE OF THEIR PARTICULAR SKILLS AND PASSIONS...
"...AND OTHERS WILL SIMPLY CONTINUE DOING...WHATEVER IT IS THEY NORMALLY DO."

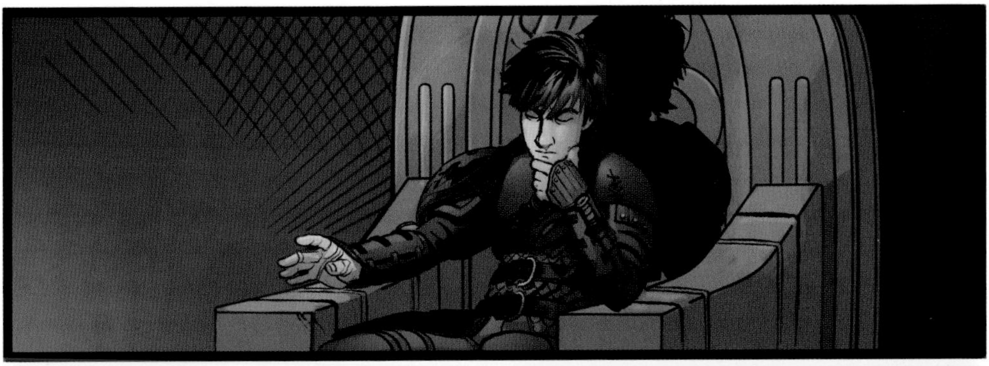

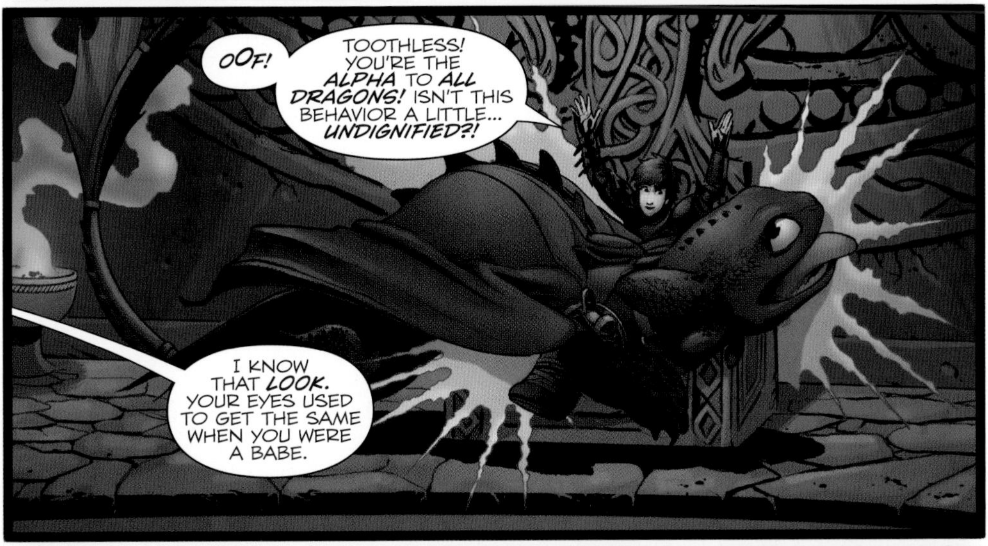
OOF!
TOOTHLESS! YOU'RE THE ALPHA TO ALL DRAGONS! ISN'T THIS BEHAVIOR A LITTLE... UNDIGNIFIED?!
I KNOW THAT LOOK. YOUR EYES USED TO GET THE SAME WHEN YOU WERE A BABE.

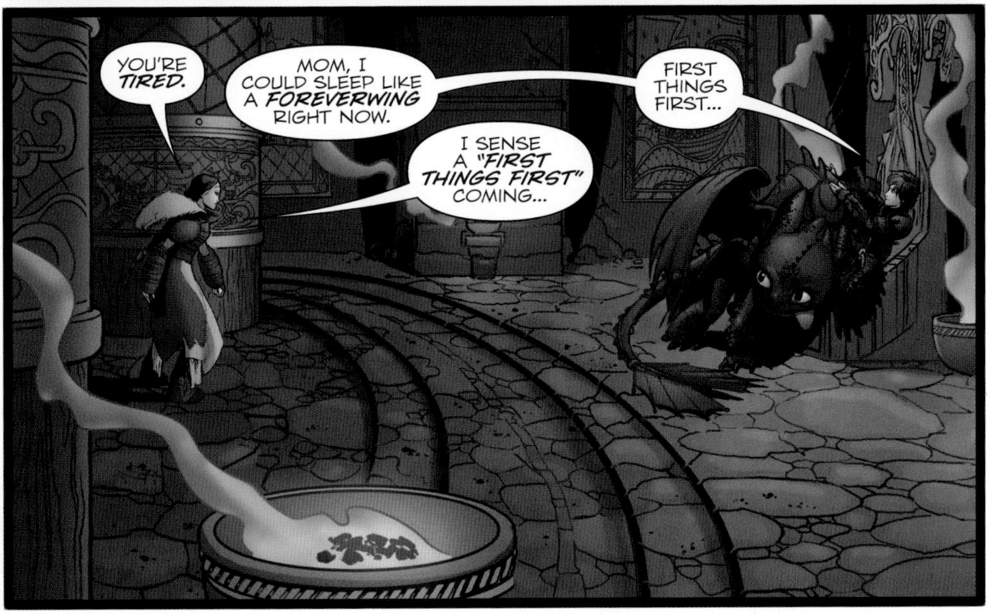
YOU'RE TIRED.
MOM, I COULD SLEEP LIKE A FOREVERWING RIGHT NOW.
FIRST THINGS FIRST...
I SENSE A "FIRST THINGS FIRST" COMING...

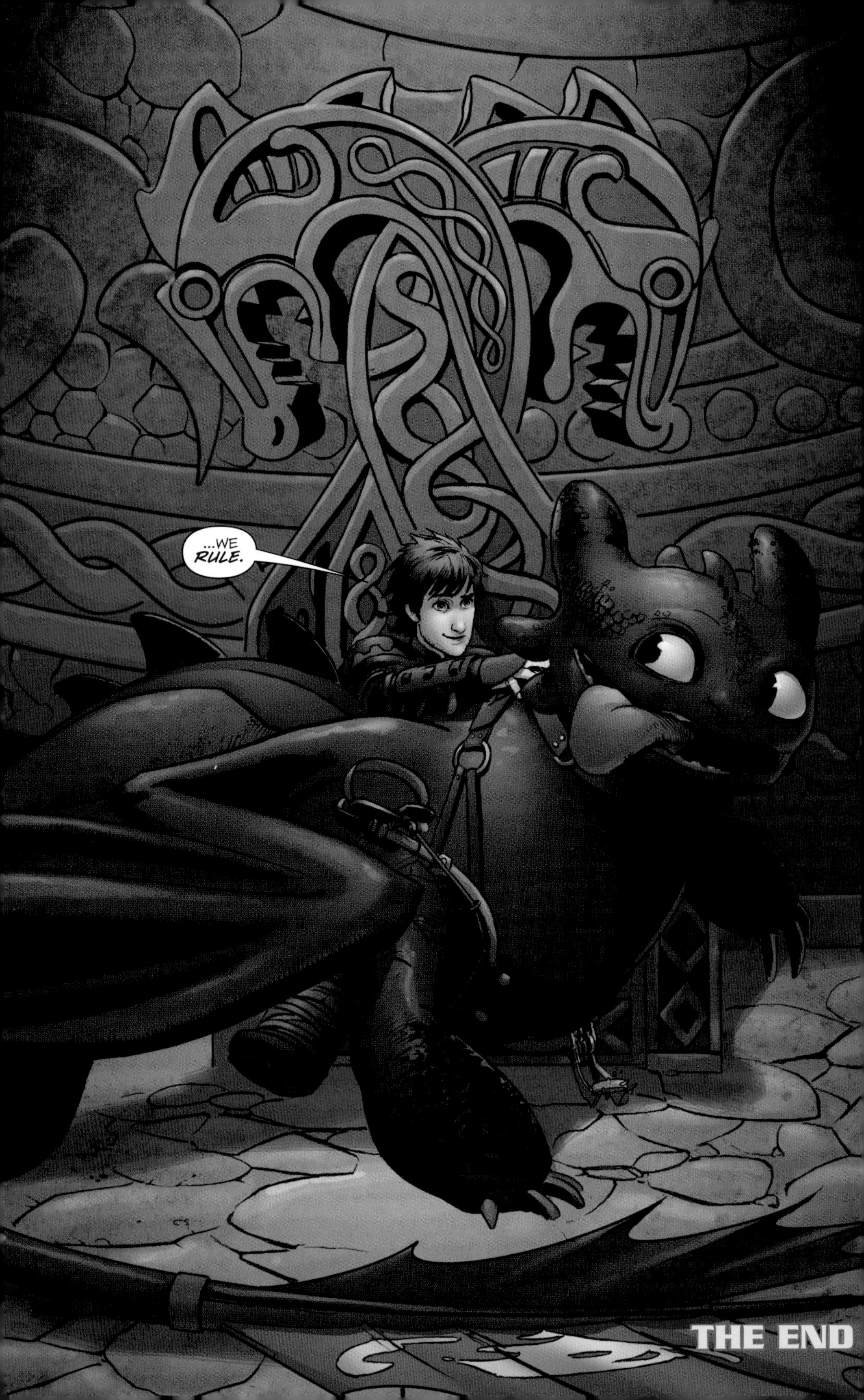
...WE *RULE.*
THE END

OTHER BOOKS FROM DARK HORSE

ITTY BITTY HELLBOY
Mike Mignola, Art Baltazar, Franco Aureliani

Witness the awesomeness that is *Hellboy*! The characters that sprung from Mike Mignola's imagination, with an AW YEAH Art Baltazar and Franco twist! This book has ALL the FUN, adventure, and AW YEAHNESS in one itty bitty package! That's a true story right there.

Volume 1: 978-1-61655-414-9 | $9.99
Volume 2: The Search for the Were-Jaguar! 978-1-61655-801-7 | $12.99

AVATAR: THE LAST AIRBENDER
Gene Luen Yang, Gurihiru

The wait is over! Ever since the conclusion of *Avatar: The Last Airbender*, its millions of fans have been hungry for more—and it's finally here! This series of digests rejoins Aang and friends for exciting new adventures, beginning with a face-off against the Fire Nation that threatens to throw the world into another war, testing all of Aang's powers and ingenuity!

THE PROMISE TPB
Book 1: 978-1-59582-811-8 | $10.99
Book 2: 978-1-59582-875-0 | $10.99
Book 3: 978-1-59582-941-2 | $10.99

THE SEARCH TPB
Book 1: 978-1-61655-054-7 | $10.99
Book 2: 978-1-61655-190-2 | $10.99
Book 3: 978-1-61655-184-1 | $10.99

THE RIFT TPB
Book 1: 978-1-61655-295-4 | $10.99
Book 2: 978-1-61655-296-1 | $10.99
Book 3: 978-1-61655-297-8 | $10.99

SMOKE AND SHADOW TPB
Book 1: 978-1-61655-761-4 | $10.99
Book 2: 978-1-61655-790-4 | $10.99
Book 3: 978-1-61655-838-3 | $10.99

THE PROMISE LIBRARY EDITION HC
978-1-61655-074-5 | $39.99

THE SEARCH LIBRARY EDITION HC
978-1-61655-226-8 | $39.99

THE RIFT LIBRARY EDITION HC
978-1-61655-550-4 | $39.99

PLANTS VS. ZOMBIES
Paul Tobin, Ron Chan

The confusing-yet-brilliant inventor known only as Crazy Dave helps his niece Patrice and young adventurer Nate Timely fend off Zomboss's latest attacks in this series of hilarious tales! Winner of over thirty Game of the Year awards, *Plants vs. Zombies* is now determined to shuffle onto all-ages bookshelves to tickle funny bones and thrill . . . *brains*.

LAWNMAGGEDON
978-1-61655-192-6 | $9.99

TIMEPOCALYPSE
978-1-61655-621-1 | $9.99

BULLY FOR YOU
978-1-61655-889-5 | $9.99

GARDEN WARFARE
978-1-61655-946-5 | $9.99

GROWN SWEET HOME
978-1-61655-971-7 | $9.99

AVAILABLE AT YOUR LOCAL COMICS SHOP OR BOOKSTORE! • To find a comics shop in your area, call **1-888-266-4226.**

For more information or to order direct visit DarkHorse.com or call 1-800-862-0052 Mon.–Fri. 9 AM to 5 PM Pacific Time • Prices and availability subject to change without notice.

DarkHorse.com Mike Mignola's Hellboy™ © Michael Mignola. Avatar: The Last Airbender © Viacom International Inc. All Rights Reserved. Nickelodeon, Nickelodeon Avatar: The Last Airbender and all related titles, logos and characters are trademarks of Viacom International Inc. Plants vs. Zombies © Electronic Arts Inc. Plants vs. Zombies, PopCap, EA, and the EA logo are trademarks of Electronic Arts Inc. Dark Horse Books® and the Dark Horse logo are registered trademarks of Dark Horse Comics, Inc. All rights reserved. (BL 6041)

DARK HORSE BOOKS

DISCOVER THE ADVENTURE!

Explore these beloved books for the entire family.

BIRD BOY
Volume 1: The Sword of Mali Mani
ISBN 978-1-61655-930-4 | $9.99

Volume 2: The Liminal Wood
ISBN 978-1-61655-968-7 | $9.99

CHIMICHANGA
ISBN 978-1-59582-755-5 | $14.99

**USAGI YOJIMBO:
TRAVELS WITH JOTARO**
ISBN 978-1-59307-220-9 | $15.99

**PLANTS VS. ZOMBIES:
LAWNMAGEDDON**
ISBN 978-1-61655-192-6 | $9.99

**SCARY
GODMOTHER**
ISBN 978-1-59582-589-6 | $24.99

AVAILABLE AT YOUR LOCAL COMICS SHOP OR BOOKSTORE

To find a comics shop in your area, call 1-888-266-4226. For more information or to order direct visit DarkHorse.com or call 1-800-862-0052.

Bird Boy™ © Anne Szabla. Chimichanga™ © Eric Powell. Plants vs. Zombies © Electronic Arts Inc. Plants vs. Zombies, PopCap, EA, and the EA logo are trademarks of Electronic Arts Inc. Scary Godmother™ © Jill Thompson. Usagi Yojimbo™ © Stan Sakai. Dark Horse Books® and the Dark Horse logo are registered trademarks of Dark Horse Comics, Inc. All rights reserved. (BL 5011)

Mike Richardson President and Publisher

Neil Hankerson Executive Vice President

Tom Weddle Chief Financial Officer

Randy Stradley Vice President of Publishing

Michael Martens Vice President of Book Trade Sales

Matt Parkinson Vice President of Marketing

David Scroggy Vice President of Product Development

Dale LaFountain Vice President of Information Technology

Cara Niece Vice President of Production and Scheduling

Nick McWhorter Vice President of Media Licensing

Ken Lizzi General Counsel

Dave Marshall Editor in Chief

Davey Estrada Editorial Director

Scott Allie Executive Senior Editor

Chris Warner Senior Books Editor

Cary Grazzini Director of Specialty Projects

Lia Ribacchi Art Director

Vanessa Todd Director of Print Purchasing

Matt Dryer Director of Digital Art and Prepress

Mark Bernardi Director of Digital Publishing

Sarah Robertson Director of Product Sales

Michael Gombos Director of International Publishing and Licensing